Georgia Through
Its Folktales

First published by O Books, 2010
O Books is an imprint of John Hunt Publishing Ltd., The Bothy, Deershot Lodge, Park Lane, Ropley,
Hants, SO24 0BE, UK
office1@o-books.net
www.o-books.net

Distribution in:

UK and Europe
Orca Book Services
orders@orcabookservices.co.uk
Tel: 01202 665432 Fax: 01202 666219
Int. code (44)

USA and Canada
NBN
custserv@nbnbooks.com
Tel: 1 800 462 6420 Fax: 1 800 338 4550

Australia and New Zealand
Brumby Books
sales@brumbybooks.com.au
Tel: 61 3 9761 5535 Fax: 61 3 9761 7095

Far East (offices in Singapore, Thailand,
Hong Kong, Taiwan)
Pansing Distribution Pte Ltd
kemal@pansing.com
Tel: 65 6319 9939 Fax: 65 6462 5761

South Africa
Stephan Phillips (pty) Ltd
Email: orders@stephanphillips.com
Tel: 27 21 4489839 Telefax: 27 21 4479879

Text copyright Michael Berman 2009

Design: Stuart Davies

ISBN: 978 1 84694 279 2

A CIP catalogue record for this book is available
from the British Library.

Printed by Digital Book Print

Georgia Through Its Folktales

With translations by
Ketevan Kalandadze
illustrations by Miranda Gray
and notes on the stories by

Michael Berman

BOOKS

Winchester, UK
Washington, USA

CONTENTS

Acknowledgements

The photo on the front cover is of a painting by an artist from the Republic of Georgia, Maka Batiashvili. To see more of her work, please visit www.maka.batiashvili.net, and if you are interested in buying any of her paintings or drawings, please visit www.caucasusarts.org.uk

All the pen and ink drawings and linocuts were produced by the illustrator Miranda Gray, who is also a member of *Maspindzeli* – a Georgian choir based in the UK.

If any copyright holders have been inadvertently overlooked, and for those copyright holders that all possible efforts have been made to contact but without success, the author will be pleased to make the necessary arrangements at the first opportunity.

Introduction

The Art of Storytelling

Storytelling is as old as humankind. Long before stories were recorded, they were entrusted to storytellers. Why did our ancestors tell stories? Historians believe storytelling was used for a number of purposes: to teach history, to settle arguments, to make sense of the world (through Creation Myths), to satisfy a need for play and entertainment, to honor supernatural forces, to communicate experiences to other humans, and to record the actions and characteristics of ancestors for future generations (through legends).

Some of the books of the Bible, such as the Song of Songs and the Book of Job, were written in dramatic storytelling form and we have documentation of storytelling from many cultures. Records of storytelling have been found in many languages, including Sanskrit, Old German, Latin, Chinese, Greek, Icelandic and Old Slavonic. The origins of storytelling, however, are even more ancient. One of our earliest surviving records is found in the Westcar Papyrus of the Egyptians in which the sons of Cheops (the pyramid builder) entertained their father with stories. The epic tale, *Gilgamesh*, which relates the story of a Sumerian king, is frequently cited in history texts as our oldest, surviving epic tale.

Both Hinduism and Buddhism made use of storytelling for teaching purposes. Hindu storytellers used story cloths from *The Ramayana* to illustrate their narratives. *The Ramayana*, the great epic tale of India, is part of the Hindu scriptures for Rama, who is believed to be an incarnation of the god Vishnu. Within the Buddhist faith, Siddhartha Gautama, the founder of Buddhism, incorporated storytelling in his teachings. *The Jataka* or birth tales are stories of previous incarnations of the Buddha. There is evidence that early Christian prophets used stories in their preaching too, but little more is known. In *Judges 9:7*, Jotham tells the people of Shechem a tale to point out the wickedness of their ruler. The Hasidic Jews also used storytelling in introducing their rituals and beliefs to young children. In the *New Testament* Jesus Christ used the parable form in his teachings. Even today, storytelling remains a part of Christian services, especially for young children and for use in Sunday schools.

In fact, all the major religious traditions have made use of metaphorical stories to communicate their teachings - the stories from early India, Greek fables, Zen, Sufi, and Hasidic tales - as they have long been recognized as a means of bypassing the set attitudes and limitations of the conscious mind. Stories not only entertain; they can also alter our experience so as to facilitate growth and change.

From an educational point of view, storytelling engages the imagination, promotes language development, encourages reading, teaches people about other cultures, and helps them to understand both themselves and others.

When we listen to a story the heart rate changes, the eyes dilate, the muscles contract, and in a safe way, we really do confront witches, overcome monsters, fall in love, and find our way out of dark forests. Storytelling uses the left brain's functions (language, a story line, sequences of cause and effect) to speak the right brain's language of symbolic, intuitive, imaginative truths. For example, the small bird sits on the shoulder of the boy lost in the woods and tells him how to go home. The left brain says, "I understand the words, but birds don't speak." The right brain says, "What did the boy say back to the bird?" It understands these impossible developments as facts. In this way storytelling helps the brain to integrate its two sides into a whole, which promotes health and self-realization.

As people listen to stories, they form images in their minds

2

that are stored in the memory as symbols. Studies have shown that humans retain only 20% of what they read, but they recall 80% of symbols, which helps to explain why stories can have such a powerful impact on us.

Storytelling traditionally begins with a "Once upon a time..." opening and then a storyteller's silent pause to gather his / her thoughts. The traditional openings, of which there are many, were "rituals" that served as a signal that the teller was suspending "time and space" as we know it and transporting the audience to a world of imagination and play. (In Georgian tales, the convention generally employed was "There was, there was, and yet there was not".) Such openings not only served to identify the teller, but also to establish the audience's commitment to accept for the moment that imaginary world and its "rules". Similar "rituals" also signal the end of the story and their return to reality. However, many adults today have forgotten these "rules of the game".

Intertextuality in literature refers to the way in which a text may invoke other texts and is based on Bakhtin's idea that every utterance has some kind of dialogic relationship with other utterances which have preceded it. The opening "once upon a time" provides an example of this as it brings to mind other fairy tales that are part of our pool of knowledge and gives us an indication of what type of story to expect.

A common feature of religious rhetoric is known as the call and response – when the congregation echoes the words of the preacher or even add words of their own. This device can be made use of to actively engage listeners in the storytelling process and is a common feature of Jamaican storytelling, where the storyteller calls "Anansi" (a character that frequently appears in Jamaican tales) and the listeners respond "Story". In certain Gypsy communities another storytelling convention is made use of. To ensure an attentive audience while telling a story, the storyteller interrupts the narrative to interpolate the word "shoes"; and unless the listeners immediately respond "socks", breaks off the tale without finishing it! Storytelling can be regarded as an activity shared by storyteller and story listeners. It is the interaction of the two that makes a story "come to life" so it is a good idea to create as many opportunities as possible for this to take place.

Can a story with no identifiable author written or told in vernacular language, be considered to be literary? It would seem to go against the generally accepted idea that literary language represents the best or most prestigious forms of English, and is distinctly different from everyday usage. What counts as art is influenced by conceptions of "literature", which often means printed fiction (poetry, plays and novels), even though in practice language often combines with other media to produce artistic effects. Particular cultures place value on different kinds of English language art. Oral literature has unfortunately lost much of its currency in the dominant literate society of England. But in other cultures, such as in the Caribbean, there are highly regarded forms of storytelling with stylistic features deriving from their oral delivery.

Can a case be made for including folktales in a canon? A canon is the identification of a body of indispensable and authoritative writings. Such texts have always been important for definitions of what counts as Standard English. Samuel Johnson, for example, based his dictionary on books which he believed illustrated authoritative uses and meanings of the language. The traditional canon relies exclusively on the printed word and assumes a distance between writer and reader. Most folktales do not fit this description. However, literature in a canon, which is a pool of shared knowledge, can have a bonding purpose. People can respond to references to it, as to other shared cultural texts such as fairy tales, and this definition could justify the inclusion of folktales in such a collection.

Whether folktales can be considered to be literary or not is clearly debatable. However, we can say without any doubt at all that stories offer us doorways into new ways of seeing and being in the world, and surely there can be no greater justification for using them than that. Let us now turn our attention to where the stories in this particular collection come from, and what it is that is so special about the region.

Where the Stories Come From

Bounded by Russia to the north and northeast, Azerbaijan to the east, the Black Sea to the west, and Armenia and Turkey to the south, Georgia or *Sakartvelo* ("the homeland of the Kartvelians"– which is how the Georgians refer to themselves) is a land of myths and tales as tall as the peaks themselves … In Armenia, Noah's Ark lies on the borders. In Azerbaijan, the Garden of Eden is said to lurk somewhere in the south. Georgia is not to be outdone. If her neighbors boast of the genesis of man, Georgia claims to have been home to the gods. Prometheus was bound to one of her great peaks, his liver torn daily by the circling birds of prey (Griffin, 2001, p.2).

Not only that, for, according to traditional Georgian accounts, Georgians are descendants of Thargamos, the great-grandson of Japhet, son of the Biblical Noah (and Thargamos is the Torgom of Armenian tradition). Moreover, the ancient name of Georgia was Colchis, which was associated for centuries with the Greek myth of Jason and his 50 Argonauts, who sailed from Greece to Colchis to capture the Golden Fleece. The legend describes how Medea, the daughter of the King of Colchis, assisted Jason in his adventure, but in the end was deserted by him. It should therefore come as no surprise that Georgia contains such a rich source of traditional tales, as this collection reveals. It should also come as no surprise that the stories are the products of so many different influences–including pagan, Christian and

Islamic–in view of the troubled history of the land.

As for Georgia today, including the separatist regions of Abkhazia and South Ossetia, it has an area of 25,900 square miles and a population of about four and a half million.

Most ethnic Georgians (who constitute more than 80 percent of the population, according to the 2002 census) at least nominally associate themselves with the Georgian Orthodox Church (GOC). The Armenian Apostolic Church (AAC), the Roman Catholic Church (RCC), Judaism, and Islam traditionally have coexisted with Georgian Orthodoxy. Some religious groups are correlated with ethnicity. Azeris comprise the second largest ethnic group (approximately 285,000, or 7 percent of the population) and are largely Muslim; most live in the south-eastern region of Kvemo Kartli, where they constitute a majority. Armenians are the third largest ethnic group (estimated at 249,000, or 6 percent of the population), comprising the majority in the southern Samtskhe-Javakheti region, and largely belong to the AAC (taken from Georgia. International Religious Freedom Report 2007 Released by the Bureau of Democracy, Human Rights, and Labor. www.state.gov/g/drl/rls/irf/2007/90176.htm [accessed 1/4/08].

Although the constitution recognizes the special role of the GOC in the country's history, it also stipulates the independence of the church from the state. In theory, freedom of religion is protected by the Criminal Code, which specifically prohibits interference with worship services, persecution of a person based on religious faith or belief, and interference with the establishment of a religious organization. In practice, however, local Orthodox priests and teachers in State schools have shown themselves to be openly critical of minority religious groups and interfaith marriages, with some even actively discouraging Orthodox followers from interaction with students who belong to other churches. As for religious education in schools, an elective course on religion in society is offered, but the primary textbook approved for use on the course deals exclusively with the theology of Orthodox Christianity.

Despite the fact that Georgia has frequently been invaded by people from outside Europe, including Arabs, Armenians, Turks, Iranians, and Mongols, the people have somehow been able to retain their identity. This can be attributed in part to the inaccessibility of the mountainous regions of the country, and in part to the unique Georgian language and alphabet. Kartuli, the Georgian language, is part of the Ibero-Caucasian family of languages and is distinct from Indo-European, Turkic, and Semitic languages. It does not have any connection to other Northern Caucasian language groups either, even though it resembles them phonetically.

Above all, however, the way in which the Georgians have been able to resist being assimilated into alien cultures can probably be attributed to their Orthodox Christian faith, the faith that the people resolutely held on to even when forbidden from openly practicing it in Soviet times. As in other former Soviet states, that faith is now flourishing perhaps as never before. However, the situation was undoubtedly once very different, as we know from the traditional folktales of the people as well as from the pagan rites that are still being performed in the country even today.

Georgia, Shamanism, and the Shamanic Story

As the hot lamb's blood congealed on her hands, a young woman responded to the questions of a curious visitor. We were standing on the banks of the St'ekura, in the northeast Georgian province of Xevsureti, in the one part of the territory of Xaxmat'i's Jvari not off-limits to females. Not even a hundred kilometers as the crow flies from Tbilisi, we were in a part of Georgia very few Georgians, even now, ever visit; without electricity or all-season roads, it remains an eerily archaic outpost on the remote periphery of Europe. On a chilly July morning, the woman had come to Xevsureti's most sacred shrine, lamb in tow, to undergo the cleansing ritual known as *ganatvla*. She knelt before the priest (*xucesi*) as he intoned a prayer of benediction and healing, invoking St. George, his female partner Samdzimari, and a host of saints, angels and "children of God" (*xvtissvilni*). He extracted his dagger, and slit the lamb's throat. Its blood spilled forth onto the woman's arms, coating them up to the elbow. Following the ancient principle that the good blood of a slaughtered animal drives out the bad blood of female impurity, she hoped that the sacrifice would free her of certain "impediments" (*dabrk'olebebi*) in her life's course. She saw no contradiction between this ritual and the canons of the Orthodox Church;

8

both were integral parts of her Christian faith, both marked her as a Georgian and as a believer (*morc'mune*) (Tuite, 2004, pp.1-2).

According to Charachidzé, the religious system of the northeast Georgian, with its incorporation of Christian symbols and saints in a distinctly non-Christian matrix is "a sombre toute entière voici bientôt trente ans, ne laissant derrière elle que de faibles remous vite disparus" (Charachidzé, 1968, p.717). However, in view of the above description provided by Tuite, this would now appear to be an overly gloomy assessment of the current state of affairs, at least as far as this particular part of the country is concerned. Not surprisingly, it is not a state of affairs that the majority of "civilized" Georgians, aspiring to become future members of the E.U., are particularly keen on telling the rest of the world about, which is probably one of the reasons why so little is known about it outside the Caucasus.

It has been said on the subject of Huichol shamanism that "[I]t is the diaspora Huichols who, if they want to maintain their cultural identity, need the knowledge and services of a knowledgeable shaman even more than their cousins in the mountains, whose physical isolation has helped to preserve cultural and religious integrity to so remarkable degree" (Furst, 1994, p.164-1650). The same observation can be applied to Georgian healing practices too. However, there is currently little evidence of much interest in these practices, either among the city dwellers in Georgia itself or among diaspora Georgians in other countries, whose first port of call in times of crisis is more likely to be the Georgian Orthodox Church.

Despite the reluctance to accept this aspect of their culture by many Georgians, others have made attempts to identify shamanism in the Caucasus, as Tuite (2004) points out. For example, Nioradze (1940) likened Abkhazian and Georgian "soul-returning" rituals to similar practices performed by Buryat shamans, Bleichsteiner (1936) made ethnographic descriptions from the highland provinces of northeast Georgia available (which were subsequently cited by Eliade in his seminal work on shamanism), and Ochiauri (1954) situated the khevsur institution of oracles (*kadagi*) in Shternberg's evolutionary sequence of stages of divine election, of which Siberian shamanism represents a more primitive manifestation. And as for Charachidzé (1968, 1995), he has defined the khevsuri *kadagi* as "chamane", and interprets legendary accounts of past oracles as evidence that until recently the northeast Georgian highlanders had the practice of a "shamanic quest", through which the practitioner received his powers.

Consequently, in the light of all this evidence, the suggestion there is a shamanic tradition in Georgia is not at all far-fetched, and it can be found reflected in the folktales from the region. Bilocation (the apparent ability to be in two places at the same time), having animal familiars and/or healing powers, under-taking spiritual journeys, carrying out soul retrievals, and practicing divination, are all elements to be found the stories chosen for inclusion in this collection, and they are also all elements typically associated with shamanism.

A shaman is understood to be someone who performs an ecstatic (in a trance state), imitative, or demonstrative ritual of a séance (or a combination of all three), at will (in other words, whenever he or she chooses to do so), in which aid is sought from beings in (what are considered to be) other realities generally for healing purposes or for divination—both for individuals and/or the community.

As for the practice of shamanism, it is understood to encompass a personalistic view of the world, in which life is seen to be not only about beliefs and practices, but also about relation-ships—how we are related, and how we relate to each other. In shamanism the notion of interdependence "is the idea of the kinship of all life, the recognition that nothing can exist in and of itself without being in relationship to other things, and therefore that it is insane for us to consider ourselves as essentially unrelated parts of the whole Earth" (Halifax in Nicholson, (comp.), 1987, p.220). And through neurotheology, this assertion so often heard expressed in neo-shamanic circles that all life is connected, can now be substantiated. This is because

it has been shown that during mystical ecstasy (or its equivalent, entheogenic shamanic states [states induced by ingesting hallucinogens]), the individual experiences a blurring of the boundaries on the ego and feels at "one with Nature"; the ego is no longer confined within the body, but extends outward to all of Nature; other living beings come to share in the ego, as an authentic communion with the total environment, which is sensed as in some way divine (Ruck, Staples, et al., 2007, p.76).

The peculiar interconnectedness of communities through ties of family and obligation found in Georgian society would suggest that this is a concept that Georgians are more than familiar with. Rather than being a product of Soviet rule, the sharing or pooling resources and wealth has long been practiced by the people. It has also served to sustain them through the recent hardships they have had to endure.

Some shamanic stories consist of accounts of journeys undertaken by shamans on behalf of their clients. *Dead All Day, Every Day*, for example, could be interpreted as an account of a journey to the Upper World, by the wife of the hero for the hero, to bring about healing.

The shamanic story can be defined as a story that has either been based on or inspired by a shamanic journey, or one that contains a number of the elements typical of such a journey. Like other genres, it has "its own style, goals, entelechy, rhetoric, developmental pattern, and characteristic roles" (Turner, 1985, p.187), and like other genres it can be seen to differ to a certain extent from culture to culture. Characteristics typical of the genre include the way in which the stories all tend to contain embedded texts (often the account of the shamanic journey itself), and how the number of actors is clearly limited as one would expect in subjective accounts of what can be regarded as inner journeys. The stories also tend to be used for healing purposes – through the way in which they can free the reader from a debilitating self-image by focusing on his/her consciousness instead on a world of supernatural power. Additionally, through the use of narrative, shamans are able to provide their patients "with a language, by means of which unexpressed, and otherwise inexpressible, psychic states can be expressed" (Lévi-Strauss, 1968, p.198). Temporal dislocation and "the alteration or the transmutation of space" (Eliade, 1981, p.10) are themes that appear over and over again in shamanic stories too. Finally they are all examples of what Jürgen Kremer, transpersonal psychologist and spiritual practitioner, called "tales of power" after one of Carlos Castaneda's novels. He defines such texts as "conscious verbal constructions based on numinous experiences in non-ordinary reality, which guide individuals and help them to integrate the spiritual, mythical, or archetypal aspects of their internal and external experience in unique, meaningful, and fulfilling ways" (Kremer, 1988, p.192). In other words, they are teaching tales.

Although the traditional Georgian religion is commonly described as polytheistic, in fact this is a fallacy as there is a clear distinction between the Supreme God (*Morige Ghmerti*), creator and sustainer of the universe, and all other divine beings, as there is in other so-called polytheistic religions such as Yoruba. And many of the deities have taken on Christian names, as is the case with Santeira in Brazil for example, so that as in some parts of Europe what we find is that the worship of particular saints was actually founded upon the worship of pagan deities. Among the principal figures, for example, are "St. George" (*tsminda Giorgi*), the "Archangel".

According to ancient Georgian cosmology, as is frequently the case among indigenous peoples who practice shamanism, the universe is believed to consist of three superimposed worlds. They are: "(1) the space above the earth (the celestial world); (2) the earthly space (the surface of the earth); (3) the space below the earth (the netherworld). On the highest level are the gods; on the lowest, the demons and dragons; between the two, in the middle world, men, animals, plants, etc" (Bonnefoy, 1993, p.255).

What was once widely practiced in Georgia is perhaps best described as a revealed religion, not one that was revealed at the beginning of historical time by means of speech that has been preserved orally or in writing, as is the case with Judaism or Islam, but one that is made manifest each time the soul of a human being is possessed by a *Hat'i* (a divinity). That person, who is then regarded as being officially possessed, becomes a sort of shaman and is known as a *Kadagi*. "When the *Kadagi* goes into trance, on the occasion of a religious ritual or an event marking individual or collective life, he speaks, and it is then the god who is speaking through his mouth" (Bonnefoy, 1993, p.255). The priest-sacrificer is similarly chosen by what can be termed divine election made manifest through possession. His function, however, is multi-purpose, not only to perform rites but also to act as the political and military chief of the community.

Acting as a psychopomp, a deliverer of souls, is another role traditionally undertaken by the shaman. Contact with the souls of the dead is entrusted to the female mesultane ("she who is with the souls"), whereas the male kadagi (oracle) requires the services of Samdzimari to make the connection. And mgebari (escorts) would take on the role of accompanying the newly deceased to the "Land of Souls", more commonly known in shamanic cosmologies as the Land of the Dead.

What we can see from all this is that shamanism, albeit under different names, and in various forms, has thrived for millennia, and it has to be said that it is hard to imagine a tradition surviving for so long in so many cultures unless there were effective components to it (see Walsh, 2007, pp.120). Moreover, most of the stories in this collection, as we shall see, have their roots in this tradition.

The fact that shamanism has survived for so long and is still flourishing in certain parts of the world, either in its indigenous forms or as neo-shamanism, shows that even if it is necessary to adopt new technological inventions in order to compete with other nations and to survive in this world, it does not mean that it is necessary to adopt the religion (or the lack of it) and the civilization of the inventors, wholesale.

There is, however, as Dr Steven Sutcliffe has observed, a status hierarchy built into religious taxonomy as a result of which 'World Religion' is "disguised and reproduced as a neutral taxonomy". This has the effect of distorting the religious field and "sets up a kind of league table of religious entities" (see the post-graduate student report by Hanna Rumble in BASR *Bulletin* No 113 Nov 2008). The inevitable consequence of this is that some religions are clearly considered to be more "important" than others and thus more "worthy" of serious study and even of being practiced in the eyes of some. This clearly applies to most forms of paganism, including shamanism, and is why those of us who are "insiders" have such an important role to play in attempting to counter this unfortunate state of affairs. It is hoped that this book can represent one small step along that path.

Before moving on to look at the stories themselves, one final point should perhaps be made so as to place their importance in perspective, for in Abkhazia, and the North Caucasus in general, tales were never just "something to amuse the children".

They were traditionally one of the chief forms of enter-tainment, particularly in the mountain districts, together with music, singing and dancing. At the many feasts (i.e. elaborate meals, with much drinking and toasting), the guests would be expected to make a contribution to the entertainment, possibly in the form of a poem or a story. Relating tales would also be a feature of gatherings for the purpose of communal work. Although the primary purpose may have been entertainment, the stories also had an educational value: to confirm the community values of loyalty, hard work, hospitality and so on (Bgazhba, 1985, p.2)

As for the translations, what makes them special is the fact that the stories have been translated direct from Georgian into English, rather than from Georgian to Russian to English, which has often been the case in the past. It will also be noticed that sometimes the present tense has been used to refer to past time. This is not an oversight on the part of the translator, but intentional, as it is a device that can be used when storytelling in Georgian for dramatic effect and it has been used here for the same purpose in the English.

Bibliography

Bgazhba, Kh.S. (1985) *Abkhazian Tales*, Translated from the Russian, with new Introduction by D.G. Hunt. (Russian edition published by Alashara Publishing House, Sukhumi).

Bleichsteiner, R. (1936) Rossweihe und Pferdererennen in Totenkult der kaukasi-schen Völker. Wiener Beiträge zur Kulturgeschichte und Linguistik IV:413-495.

Bonnefoy, Y. (comp.) (1993) *American, African and Old European Mythologies*, Chicago and London, The University of Chicago Press.

Charachidzé, G. (1968) *Le système religieux de la Géorgie païenne: analyse structurale d'une civilization*, Paris: Maspero.

Eliade, M. (1981) *Tales of the Sacred and the Supernatural*, Philadelphia: The Westminster Press.

Furst, P.T. (1994) 'Persistence and Change in Huichol Shamanism' In Seaman, G., & Day, J.S. *Ancient Traditions: Shamanism in Central Asia and the Americas*, Boulder, Colorado: University Press of Colorado.

Griffin, N. (2001) *Caucasus: In the Wake of Warriors*, London: Headline Book Publishing.

Kremer, J.W. (1988) 'Shamanic Tales as Ways of Personal Empowerment.' In Gary Doore (ed.) *Shaman's Path: Healing, Personal Growth and Empowerment*, Boston, Massachusetts: Shambhala Publications. Pp.189-199.

Lévi-Strauss, C. (1968) *Structural Anthropology*, Harmondsworth: Penguin.

Nioradze, G. (1940) Micvalebulis haerze damarxva. ENIMKI-s moambe V-VI: 57-81.

Ochiauri, T. (1954) Kartvelta udzvelesi sarc'munoebis ist'oriidan (From the history of the ancient religion of the Georgians) Tbilisi: Mecniereba.

Ruck, Carl A.P., Staples, B.D., Celdran J.A.G., Hoffman, M.A.

(2007) *The Hidden World: Survival of Pagan Shamanic Themes in European Fairytales*, North Carolina: Carolina Academic Press.

Tuite, K. (2004) 'Highland Georgian paganism — archaism or innovation?' Review of Zurab K'IK'NADZE 1996, *Kartuli Mitologia,I. Δvari da saq'mo*. (Georgian Mythology, I. The cross and his people [*sic*], Kutaisi: Gelati Academy of Sciences; for the Annual of the Society for the Study of the Caucasus. http://www.mapageweb.umontreal.ca/tuitekj/publications/Shamanism Acetates.pdf. [accessed 29/10/07]

Turner, V. (1985) *On the Edge of the Bush: Anthropology as Experience*. Tucson, AZ: University of Arizona Press.

Walsh, R.N. (2007) *The World of Shamanism: New Views of an Ancient Tradition*, Woodbury, Minnesota: Llewellyn Publications.

Dead All Day, Every Day

We know that celestial phenomena have interested Georgians since ancient times from the Georgian sayings and legends that have been passed down which mention such matters. The principal thought or moral of such legends was the "supremacy of celestial laws" and the "inevitability of punishment by powerful celestial forces." The ancient Georgians attached a mystical character to the sky and to celestial phenomena, thereby acknowledging their full grandeur.

Archaeological evidence of the importance that the ancient Georgians attached to the sun and the moon has also been unearthed. In the 1940s, for example, approximately thirty massive bronze plates were discovered dating from the 16-14th centuries BC. They were found primarily in the graves of women at various burial sites, including the large burial ground known as "Zadengora," and their surfaces are covered by numerous convex, circular apertures – images of the Sun and Moon.

Worship of the cults of fire, heat, and light clearly played an important role in the lives of the Georgian tribes that populated the eastern regions of Georgia at that time. Giving tribute to the Sun as the principal source of light and heat and also seeing its large dimensions, the ancient masters and artists depicted it in the centre of the bronze plates in the form of a circular aperture. The Moon served as another important source of light for the ancients, and it can be seen depicted on the bronze plates in the form of sickle-shaped apertures (This information on the archeological evidence that has been unearthed was taken from "The Unknown History of Georgian Astronomy" http://www.as.wvu.edu/~scmcc/simonia.txt [accessed 30/12/07]).

The following tale, about the punishment meted out by the Sun on someone who dared to disrespect him, was collected by the eminent Georgian folklorist Elene Virsaladze and comes from

Folktales of the World: Georgian Folktales, published in 1984 in Tbilisi by Nakaduli Publishing. It has been translated into English by Ketevan Kalandadze.

It is interesting to note that in the Turkic world on the borders of Georgia the sun is conceived as female, as it is in this particular tale, and the moon as male. However, under the influence of outside religious beliefs, this is sometimes found to be reversed, as in Western culture (see Van Deusen, 2004, p.179).

There was a merchant who had three daughters. One day, before he set off on one of his long business trips, he brought his daughters to him and told them:

"I'm going far away for a year. Tell me what I can bring you back."

"I want a dress that will put itself on and take itself off," said the oldest daughter.

"I'd like a mirror which can show me what's going on all over the world," said the middle daughter.

Then the merchant asked his youngest daughter:

"And what should I bring you back?"

The youngest daughter said:

"I need to think about it and will let you know later."

The girl had a very clever nanny and asked her:

"My father's going to a faraway country. What should I ask him to bring me back from there?"

The nanny said:

"Ask your father to bring you the magic apple that will make all your dreams come true."

The girl went to her father and asked him:

"Bring me the kind of apple that when I eat a piece of it, it will make all my wishes come true, and then become whole once again."

The father agreed and went on his journey. He returned a year later with the presents for the oldest and the middle daughters, but to the youngest he said:

"I couldn't find your magic apple. I was told that there is a garden in the East with a gate of snakes and it's guarded by fierce dragons. The apple tree grows in that garden but no human has ever visited it. Nobody has ever touched that tree so how on earth could I have brought it back for you? I'm sorry but it just wasn't possible."

The girl was very upset and started to cry. Her nanny came and asked:

"Why are you crying, my sweetie?"

"My father came back with the presents for my sisters, but not for me, and he said he couldn't get what I asked him for."

"Not to worry, you can get it yourself if you're determined enough," the nanny said. "Get yourself ready and journey eastwards. Keep going until you get to the field with nothing growing in it. There you will see a tiny garden with a gate of snakes and two dragons guarding it. There's only one apple tree in that garden. At midday, when the sun is at its strongest, the

snakes and dragons fall asleep. You need to be ready exactly then. Run into the garden, pick one of the apples, and then return again, as quickly as you can, without ever looking back behind you."

So the girl set off on the journey, doing exactly what her nanny had advised her to do. She walked for one day, two days, three days, and after walking for a month she eventually reached the field. There she saw a gate entwined with snakes, and, at the entrance, two dragons with their mouths open. In the middle of the garden she saw only one tree, made of silver with emerald leaves and big juicy apples. On one side of the tree all the apples were a ruby color, and on the other side a diamond color.

Seeing all those apples made the girl more determined than ever to get to the tree. She said to herself - I'm still going to try to get my apple whatever will happen to me.

She waited till midday and then, when she got close to the garden, she saw that the snakes and dragons were asleep. She rushed into the garden, picked an apple and then ran away again, just as quickly as she could. She is very happy but then she hears some noise coming from behind her. She looks back and sees that all the snakes from the gate and the dragons are coming after her. What can she do? Can she climb up a tree perhaps? But that won't help her. There is no way out. It is impossible to get away from them. She runs and runs, and when she reaches the field with nothing growing in it, she hears a voice:

"Leave that apple or die."

The desperate girl throws the apple back and falls unconscious. In a little while, she comes to again and looks around, but there is nothing there – no apple, no snakes, and no dragons. She is in the middle of the field. She wants to go back home but she cannot find the way. In the end she starts walking, but has not got a clue where she is going. Suddenly she sees a tiny chapel. She has a look around but finds it is locked from inside. What can she do? She starts crying. She has no food or shelter. She sits down nearby and soon it gets dark. She hears a noise from inside the chapel, gets very frightened and hides. The door of the church opens and a young man comes out and disappears into the dark. He leaves the door open, so the girl goes in and sees that in one corner there is a coffin and in another there is a bed. In front of the bed there is a small table laid for a meal with bread and wine. The girl is very hungry and wants to have some of the bread, but suddenly someone comes in and the girl hides under the bed. The young man walks up and down, washes his hands, sits down and eats the bread himself.

As soon as dawn comes, the young man opens the lid of the coffin and lies down inside it.

The girl comes out of hiding, goes to the coffin to ask the man for some bread, but the man is already dead. She gets scared but she decides in any case to take the bread without asking. She goes to the table, sits down to eat, but is very surprised because despite the fact that she had seen the young man eat the bread, everything on the table is somehow still untouched. After that she cannot find the courage to eat the bread. So she is still very hungry but has not eaten or touched anything. She opens the door because she wants to leave, but where can she go? She cannot see any path that would lead her back to her home.

She wanders around for a while and in the evening she returns to the chapel again. When the sun goes down, the church lights come on all by themselves. She looks at the coffin and hears some noise coming from inside. She is frightened and hides behind the bed again. The young man climbs out of the coffin, washes his hands and face, goes to the table and starts eating the bread. Some crumbs fall down on to the floor so the girl sticks her hand out from under the bed, catches a few and eats them. After that, she is not so hungry any more.

In the morning the man gets back into his coffin again. He has not noticed the girl at all. The girl then comes out of hiding and decides to eat. She gets to the table and sees that everything is still untouched, the same as on the previous day. She is very surprised because she saw with her own eyes that he was eating. She cuts a slice of bread and some meat and eats. She also pours herself a glass of wine and drinks it.

When it gets dark she goes under the bed again. The young man climbs out of the coffin and goes to the table. But he jumps up with surprise when he sees the bread.

"What's happening to me? I've been here for 30 years now and in all that time I've never seen even one mouse here."

He cuts a big slice of bread and throws it on the floor; the girl tries to take it. The man then grabs hold of her hand and pulls her out from under the bed. He sees a beautiful woman and likes her a lot.

They tell each other their life stories. The girl asks him:

"Why is it that you are dead during the day and alive at night?"

The man tells her his story:

"I was the son of a nobleman and I loved hunting. One day I spotted a deer and I followed it all day and night. It went up a high hill and after that I couldn't see her again. When I was going up the hill, the sun was looking down on to the earth with all his nine eyes, so it was unbearably hot and I was very tired. With my bow and arrow I shot at the sun and hit him in his ninth eye. Since then there has always been darkness in one of the countries of this world. Because of this, God punished me and sent this curse – that I am dead all day every day, and only alive at night. For this reason I can't live together with my relatives, and that's why my parents built this small chapel for me, in this field. They put my coffin in here and I've been here ever since.

I've been allocated a fixed amount of food - one loaf of bread, one portion of lamb, and one bottle of wine. When I pour the wine from the bottle it gets filled up again, the same happens with the bread and the meat I eat. But you see the slice you cut from the bread stays eaten. What can I do with you? What can I feed you with?"

They both started to cry and finally the boy said:

"Not to worry. I'd like you to stay with me despite that."

They fell in love with each other. And the boy would disappear every night, to bring her some bread. Sometimes he would even give her his portion while he went hungry for her. He spent six months looking after her like this.

The girl was pregnant and it became noticeable.

"I love you very much, as you know, but it's impossible for you to stay with me any longer, especially now you're pregnant," said the man.

The girl started to cry:

"I cannot possibly leave you now," she said.

But the boy persuaded her to. He gave her a ball of thread and threw it into the field

"Follow it and stop when it stops. It will bring you to my parents' home but don't tell them anything about me... you will have a baby, then you can leave the baby there and come back to me," he said.

He kissed the girl and let her go.

The girl is following the ball, and the ball stops in front of a castle. The girl sat down nearby and the servants saw her. At first they wanted to get rid of her, but then the old owner of the house saw her, took pity on the pregnant girl and let her enter the castle. The girl lived there from that day onwards, and one day she gives birth to a beautiful son.

The poor girl is lying on the floor covered with hay and all her clothes are torn. At nights someone comes to her and talks.

"My poor soul, how are you, and how is my son?"

"We are lying on a bed of hay, wearing torn clothes, only have stale crusts of bread to eat, and one glass of water that I use to soften the bread in."

The man from outside says:

"My poor mother, my poor father and my poor nanny!"

The servants heard all this, went and told the owner:

"Someone comes to the girl at night and says these words."

One night the house owners themselves went and hid themselves in the corner of the girl's room. At night the man came as usual and said:

"My poor soul, how are you and how is my son?"

"We are lying on a bed of hay, wearing torn clothes, only have stale crusts of bread to eat, and one glass of water that I use to soften the bread in."

"My poor mother, my poor father and my poor nanny!"

The house owners ran out of the house but could not see anyone. They asked the girl who was speaking to her and she told them the whole story. They suspected that it was their son. So they moved the girl to a nice room with servants to look after her, and said:

"When our son comes don't let him go. Tell him that you want to see him. We haven't seen our dead son for so long," the parents said.

Nothing happened that night. The next night the man comes and says from outside the door.

"My poor soul, how are you and how is my son?"

"Come in, my dear," the girl replied.

"I'm not allowed to come in, I wasn't even allowed to come this far. Just tell me, how are you?"

The girl said:

"I'm not going to tell you anything. Come in and see with your own eyes."

The man could not stand the situation, being separated from his love this way, so he entered the room and started to hug his baby and wife.

His parents then came out of hiding, recognized their son, and started kissing him and crying. They did not want him to leave any more.

"Stay with us," they said.

The man said:

"It will be dawn soon and I have to leave; otherwise I will die," he was trying to explain.

And then dawn did come, and the boy collapsed and died, just as he said he would.

His parents were heartbroken and went into mourning. As for the girl, instead of just accepting the situation, she decided to do something about it.

Nobody here can help him so I need to find a cure for him myself.

She got up and left, taking four of the parents' servants with her.

She realizes that she needs to visit the sun and to find out how to heal her husband there.

She walks and walks, and the four servants follow her. She walks for months and years. Her servants die one by one. All her clothes are torn and she is very tired. She nearly loses hope of ever managing to return home again, but she is still determined to get to the land of the sun somehow and to ask there for the healing of her husband.

Finally she gets to the castle of the sun, but the sun is not at home. Instead, his mother opens the door and mutters to herself:

"I've never seen any human get here before. They're all afraid of my son because he burns everything."

The mother of the sun then says to the girl:

"How do you dare to come here? Aren't you scared?"

"No, I'm not," replied the girl. "I want to ask him something."

And she told the mother of the sun her whole story, about everything that had happened to her, and asked her to show her the sun.

"It's impossible to meet my son because he burns everything. I will tell him your problem though."

The sun's mother was a human being and she felt sorry for the girl, so she decided to help her. She gave the girl food, clothes to wear, and hid her.

That evening the sun came home, with his eyes all ablaze, and the first thing he said was:

"I smell a human!"

His mother thought quickly and answered:

"No my son. It's me. I had a bath today and changed my clothes. You forget that I'm human too."

After she said that, the sun forgot all about the matter, and they sat down to eat supper together.

"My poor son. If you hadn't lost that eye, you'd have been so beautiful. I wonder why you didn't burn the person who did that to you."

" For what he is currently going though is punishment enough. He's dead all day every day, only alive at night, and nobody has seen him for 30 years now."

"Oh, my son, my son! That's surely too much punishment for anyone!"

"Yes, mother! I'm responsible for that. He's on his own in a small chapel. He has a coffin and during the day he lies in it. At night he gets up and walks around, and then, when morning comes, he dies again."

The mother started to moan:

"I'm so sorry for him."

"Me too," the sun said, "but I can't help him."

"Is there no healing for him then?" asked the mother.

"Yes there is, but who is going to bring it to him?" the sun replied.

"What is it then?" the mother asked.

"He needs one drop of the water I wash my face with."

They finish talking about the subject after that. The following day the mother brought the water for the sun to wash his face. The sun washed his face but was a bit suspicious and said to his mother:

"Pour this water away."

The mother poured the water away, as he asked her to, but left a few drops at the bottom. The sun got up and left. The mother gave the water to the girl and also gave her some food to take with on the way, saying to her:

"Whoever you meet who is dead on your way back, touch with this water and so let them be alive again."

The girl left. She is flying like a bird to get home and, though the journey is long, it holds no fear for her, so determined is she to succeed. She sees some people buried in snow, touches them with the water, and they come alive again. She gets to her servants and they too are brought back to life once more.

And after a year, she finally reaches her home. Everyone is so happy to see her, especially when they hear that she has the cure for her husband. She touches him with the water and he comes back to life again too.

Their happiness and joy had no limit, and, as far as I know, they are still living happily together, up to this very day.

(Taken from Virsaladze, E. (1984) *Folktales of the World: Georgian Folktales*, Tbilisi: Nakaduli Publishing).

The story of St. Nino, for all its fabulous embellishments, is built on a solid foundation of fact, and we know from both history and archaeological evidence that Iberia, as Eastern Georgia was then called, adopted Christianity as its state religion about A.D.330, in the time of Constantine the Great. Prior to that, we know that sun-worship was practised by the Georgians, and the extract that follows provides evidence of this. The full account can be found in *Lives and Legends of the Georgian Saints*, selected and translated from the original texts by David Marshall Lang.

The Conversion of King Mirian, and of all Georgia with him by our holy and blessed Mother, the Apostle Nino

Let us relate the story of our holy and blessed Mother, the enlightener of all Georgia, Nino the apostle, as she herself told it on her death-bed to the believer Salome of Ujarma, daughter-in-law of King Mirian.

... One day a crowd of people set out from the town to go shopping in the great city of Mtskheta and offer sacrifices to their god Armazi. St. Nino went with them, and when they had got to the city of Mtskheta they stopped by the Bridge of the Magi. When St. Nino observed the sorcerers, fire-worshippers and seducers of the people, she wept over their sad fate and grieved for their strange customs. On the next day there was a loud noise of trumpets and a fearful uproar of shouting, and mobs of people as countless as the flowers of the field, who were rushing and jostling as they waited for the king and queen to come forth.

First came Queen Nana and then King Mirian, terrible and in great splendour. Nino asked a certain Jewish woman what all this meant. She answered that it was their custom to go up into the presence of their supreme god, who was unlike any other idol. When St. Nino heard this, she climbed up with the people to see the idol called Armazi, and placed herself near it in a crevice in the rock. There was a great noise, and the king and all the people quaked with fear before the image. Nino saw the standing figure of a man made of copper. His body was clothed

29

in a golden coat of armour, and he had a gold helmet on his head. His shoulder-pieces and eyes were made from emeralds and beryl stones. In his hand he held a sword as bright as a lightning flash, which turned round in his grasp, and nobody dared touch the idol on pain of death.

They proclaimed, "If there is anyone here who despises the glory of the great god Armazi, or sides with those Hebrews who ignore the priests of sun-worship or worship a certain strange deity who is the Son of the God of Heaven—if any of these evil persons are among us, let them be struck down by the sword of him who is feared by all the world."

When they had spoken these words, they all worshipped the idol in fear and trembling. On its right there stood another image, made of gold, with the face of a man. Its name was Gatsi, and to the left of it was a silver idol with a human face, the name of which was Gaim. These were the gods of the Georgian people.

When the blessed Nino saw this, she began to sigh towards God and shed tears because of the errors of this northern land, for the light was hidden from its people and the reign of darkness enclosed them. She lifted up her eyes to heaven and said, "O God, by Thy great might throw down these enemies of Thine, and make this people wise by Thy great mercy, so that the whole nation may worship the only God through the power of Jesus Christ Thy Son, to whom belong praise and thanks for evermore."

After St. Nino had uttered this prayer, God immediately sent winds and hurricanes out of the west, with clouds sinister and grim in appearance. The noisy roar of thunder was heard, and at sunset a wind blew with a fetid and unpleasant smell. When the crowd saw this, they ran away as fast as they could towards their homes in the city. God granted them but little time, and when they were all safely home, His anger burst fiercely out from the sinister cloud. Hail fell in lumps as big as two fists on to the abode of the idols, and smashed them into little pieces. The walls were destroyed by the terrible gale, and thrown down among the rocks. But Nino remained unharmed, watching from the same spot where she had stood at the beginning...

From St Nino's biographer, we know that the national gods of the cults of pagan Georgia were Armazi (corresponding to the Zoroastrian deity Ahura-Mazda), Zaden, Gatsi and Gaim. They were represented by idols made from precious metals and set with precious stones, and were worshipped both by the royal court at Mtskheta-Armazi as well as by the ordinary people. "Simple folk whom St Nino encountered at the town of Urbnisi worshipped the sacred fire of the Zoroastrians and also images of stone and wood; there was, too, a miracle-working tree to which the people attributed wondrous powers of healing" (Burney & Lang, 1971, p.223).

The Persians, whose rule over Asia Minor and most of Armenia lasted from 546 to 331 BC, had been inspired by the religious teaching of Zoroaster, and the worship of the Persian Armazi coalesced with the older Georgian worship of astral, solar and lunar gods, which was then subsumed into the Christian-pagan worship of St. George (see Anderson, 2003, p.143). As to why the gift of fire had been considered to be so precious, it "enabled mankind to work metal and took him out of his natural state and beyond the age of stone" (Anderson, 2003, p.171).

The worship of Armazi was closely connected with that of Kartlos, who was the hero-founder of the Kartlians. And the image of the god Armazi-Ormuzd, as described in the *Life of St. Nino*, bears a strong resemblance to the Hittite Teshub, who was also known to carry a curved sword. "[H]is worship may be connected with the sword cult of the Scythians and Alans, and with the axe-cult the indications of which are found in the remains at Koban and Kazbek. In association with Armazi were the gods Ga and Gatsi, whom the Annalists accept as the old native gods of the Georgians" (Allen, 1932, p.37).

Further evidence to indicate a Caucasian sun god was formerly worshipped in Georgia can be found, among other places, in the city of Uplistsikhe (უფლისციხე—The Fortress of the Lord), Founded in the sixteenth century BC and carved out of rock, Uplistsikhe was a bustling city over 3000 years ago and was, before the introduction of Christianity in the fourth century, a major regional centre of Caucasian pagan worship.

However, after Saint Nino converted King Mirian II of Iberia, the pagan temples of Uplistsikhe were sacked, though their remains can still be found under a church that was built in the 9th century on the site. It thus comes as no surprise that in a number of Georgian folktales we not only find the Sun and his mother personified, but the hero/heroine attempting to communicate with them on behalf of both themselves and others.

Incidentally, the influence of the Zoroastrian religion permeated Azerbaijan too, with evidence being provided in the form of *Kyz Kalazy*, the famous Maiden Tower in the old quarter of Baku. Though it has now become a trinket shop frequented by tourists, the latest archaeological research suggests that the landmark which dates from around 800 BC was originally a fire temple, and that each of its seven floors would have been devoted to a separate deity in the holy pantheon of Ahura-Mazda.

The flickering fires that flamed above the oil which seeped continuously to the surface of the ground made it the natural home of fire worship and, after the Zoroastrian religion gave way to Islam, parties of Parsees from Bombay, Indian Zoroastrians, would come to Baku to tend the "eternal flame" and conduct religious ceremonies (Anderson, 2003, p.27). There is also a Zoroastrian temple at Surakhani, set among the ubiquitous oil wells on the outskirts of Baku.

At different times different divinities have governed the world, yet in the entire course of human history the Sun has been considered the very source of everything, just as it seems to be in this particular tale. Not only have the Sun, the Moon and stars frequently been personified in stories, but people have also turned to them in prayers (as the peasant does to the Sun in this tale) and made sacrifices in their honor as well (see Sliimets, 2006, pp.129-130).

The Sumerian sun-god Utu was believed to be the enemy of darkness and evil, and to have the ability to chase away diseases with the healing power in his wings. He was also known as the god of justice, and in later times he was called Shamash, which in the Akkadian language means "sun" (see McKenzie & Prime & George & Dunning, 2001, p.24). It is interesting to observe that in our particular story, the Sun can be seen to dispense justice too, though albeit a rather cruel form of justice, at least as far as the hero is concerned.

Bibliography

Allen, W.E.D. (1932) *A History of the Georgian People*, London: Kegan Paul, Trench, Trubner & Co., Ltd.

Anderson, T. (2003) *Bread and Ashes: A Walk Through the Mountains of Georgia*, London: Jonathan Cape.

Berman, M. (2008) *The Shamanic Themes in Georgian Folktales*, Newcastle: Cambridge Scholars Publishing

Burney, C., & Lang, D.M. (1971) *The People of the Hills: Ancient Ararat and Caucasus*, London: Phoenix Press.

Lang, D.M. (1956) *Lives and Legends of the Georgian Saints*, London: George Allen & Unwin.

Sliimets, Ülo (2006) 'The Sun, the Moon and Firmament in Chukchi Mythology and on the Relations of Celestial Bodies and Sacrifice'.

http://www.folklore.ee/Folklore/vol32/siimets.pdf   [accessed 2/11/07].

Van Deusen, K. (2004) *Singing Story Healing Drum: Shamans and Storytellers of Turkic Siberia*, Montreal: McGill-Queen's University Press.

The Prince Who befriended the Beasts

The tale that follows comes from Samegrelo - a lowland region in the west of Georgia, bordering the Black Sea. Tea and grapes are the chief products of the region and Poti is the main port. It was taken from the collection of Georgian tales translated by Marjorie Wardrop and first published in 1894. The story was collected by Professor Tsagareli and first published in *Mingrelskie Etudy, S. Pbg.*, 1880.

There was a king, and he had three sons. Once he fell ill, and became blind in both eyes. He sent his son for a surgeon. All the surgeons agreed that there was a fish of a rare kind by the help of which the king might be cured. They made a sketch of the fish, and left it with the sick monarch.

The king commanded his eldest son to go and catch that fish in the sea. A hundred men with their nets were lost in the sea, but nought could they find like the fish they sought. The eldest son came home to his father and said: "I have found nothing." This displeased the king, but what could he do? Then the second son set out, taking with him a hundred men also, but all his men were lost too, and he brought back nothing.

After this, the youngest brother went. He had recourse to cunning; he took with him a hundred kilas of flour (Kila, a measure of flour = about 36-40 pounds) and one man. He came to the sea, and every day he strewed flour in the water, near the shore, until all the flour was used up; the fishes grew fat on the flour, and said: "Let us do a service to this youth since he has

35

enabled us to grow fat"; so, as soon as the youth threw a net into the sea, he at once drew out the rare fish he sought. He wrapped it up in the skirt of his robe, and went his way.

As he rode along, some distance from his companion, he heard a voice that said: "O youth, I am dying!" But on looking round he saw no man, and continued his journey. After a short time, he again heard the same words. He looked round more carefully, but saw nothing. Then he glanced at the skirt of his robe, and saw that the fish had its mouth open, and was dying. The youth said to it: "What dost thou want?" The fish answered: "It will be better for thee if thou wilt let me go, some day I shall be of use to thee." The youth took it and threw it into the water, saying to his comrade: "I hope thou wilt not betray me."

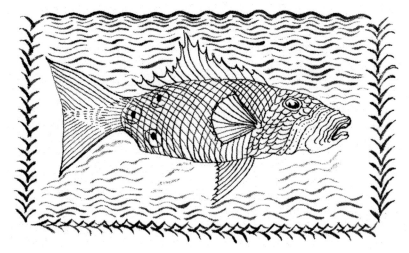

When he reached home, he told his father that he had been unsuccessful. Some time passed. Once the prince quarreled Note: You can't change this to American English spelling as it was originally published in British English with his comrade, and the latter ran off and told the king how his son had deceived him. When the king heard this, he ordered his son to be taken away and killed. He was taken out, but when they were about to kill him, the youth entreated them, saying: "What doth it profit you if you slay me? If you let me go, 'twill be a good deed, and I shall flee to foreign lands." The executioners took pity on him, and set him free; he thanked them, and departed.

He went, he went, he went, he went farther than anybody ever went – he came to a great forest. As he went through the forest, he saw a deer running, in a great state of alarm. The youth stopped, and fixed his gaze on it; then the deer came up and fell on its face before him. The youth asked: "What ails thee?" "The prince pursues me, and on thee depends my safety." The youth took the deer with him and went on. A huntsman met him, and asked: "Whither art thou leading the deer?" The youth replied: "One king has sent it as a gift to another king, and, lo! I am taking it." The youth thus saved the deer from death, and the deer said: "A time will come when I shall save thy life."

The youth went on his way: he went, he went, he went, so far he went, good sir, that the three day colt (of fable) could not go so far. He looked, and, lo! A frightened eagle perched on his shoulder, and said: "Youth, on thee depends my safety!" The youth protected it also from its pursuer. Then the eagle said to him: "Some day I shall do thee a service."

The youth went on: he went through the forest, he went, he went, he went, he went further than he could, he went a week, two weeks, a year and three months. Then he heard some fearful rumbling, roaring, thunder and lightning – something was coming through the forest, breaking down all the trees. A great jackal appeared, and ran up to the youth, saying: "If thou wilt thou canst protect me; the prince is pursuing me with all his army." The youth saved the jackal, as he had saved the other animals. Then the jackal said: "Some day I shall help thee."

The youth went on his way, and, when he was out of the wood, came to a town. In this town he found a castle of crystal, in the courtyard of which he saw a great number of young men, some dying and some dead. He asked the meaning of this, and was told: "The king of this land has a daughter, a maiden queen;

37

she has made a proclamation that she will wed him that can hide himself from her; but no man can hide himself from her, and all these men has she slain, for he that cannot hide himself from her is cast down from the top of the castle."

When the youth heard this, he at once arose, and went to the maiden. They bowed themselves each to the other. The maiden asked him: "Wherefore art thou come hither?" The youth answered: "I come for that which others have come for." She immediately called her viziers together, and they wrote out the usual contract.

The youth went out from the castle, came to the seashore, sat down, and was soon buried in thought. Just then, something made a great splash in the sea, came and swallowed the youth, carried him into the Red Sea, there they were hidden in the depths of the sea, near the shore. The youth remained there all that night.

When the maiden arose the next morning she brought her mirror and looked in it, but she found nothing in the sky, she looked on the dry land, and found nothing there, she looked at the sea – and then she saw the youth in the belly of the fish, which was hiding in the deep waters. After a short time, the fish threw up the youth on the place where it had found him. He went merrily to the maiden. She asked: "Well, then, didst thou hide thyself?" "Yes, I hid myself." But the maiden told him where he had been, and how he got there, and added: "This time I forgive thee, for the cleverness thou hast shown."

The youth set out again, and sat down in a field. Then something fell upon him, and took him up into the air, lifted him up into the sky, and covered him with its wing. When the maiden arose next morning, she looked in her mirror, she gazed at the mountain, she gazed at the earth, but she found nothing, she looked at the sky, and there she saw how the eagle was covering the youth. The eagle carried the youth down, and put him on the ground. He was joyful, thinking that the maiden could not have seen him; but when he came to her she told him all.

Then he fell into a deep melancholy, but the maiden, being struck with wonder at his cunning in hiding himself, told him that she again forgave him. He went out again, and, as he was walking in the field, the deer came to him and said: "Mount on my back." He mounted, and the deer carried him away, away, away over all the mountains that were there, and put him in a lair. When the maiden arose the next morning, she found him, and when he came back to her she said: "Young man, it seems that thou hast many friends, but thou canst not hide thyself from me; yet this day also I forgive thee." The youth went sadly away; he lost his confidence.

When he sat down in the field, an earthquake began, the town shook, lightning flashed, thunder rolled, and when a thunderbolt had fallen, there leapt out from it his friend the gigantic jackal, and said to him: "Fear not, O youth!" The jackal had recourse to his wonted cunning, it began to

scrape at the earth: it dug, it dug, it dug, and burrowed right up to the place where the maiden dwelt, and then it said to the youth: "Stay thou here, she will look at the sky, the mountain, the sea, and when she cannot find thee she will break her mirror; when thou hearest this, then strike thy head through the ground and come out."

This advice, of course, pleased the youth. When the maiden arose in the morning, she looked at the sea, she found him not, she looked at the mountain, she looked at the sky, and still she could not see him, so she broke her mirror. Then the youth pushed his head through the floor, bowed, and said to the maiden: "Thou art mine and I am thine!"

They summoned the viziers, sent the news to the king, and a great feast began.

As is so often the case in tales from the Caucasus, the story features three sons, and again, as is customary, it is the youngest of the three who succeeds in the end and is thus in a position to assume the role that his father formerly played. Initially, however, he fails in his mission and he is forced to flee for his life. On his journey, he encounters, in turn, a deer, an eagle and a jackal. The youth saves them all from danger, and in return they offer to help him whenever the need should arise.

Again and again in stories "we see how things appear in threes: how things have to happen three times, how the hero is given three wishes; how Cinderella goes to the ball three times; how the hero or the heroine is the third of three children" (Booker, 2004, p.229). Pythagoras called three the perfect number in that it represented the beginning, the middle and the end, and he thus regarded it as a symbol of Deity. Not only is the hero one of three brothers, but he also encounters three animal helpers, so the repetition of the number must surely be more than just coincidental and we are led to conclude that this features in tale for a purpose. A Trinity is not only found in Christianity, though given the fact that the Georgians are Orthodox Christians this must be the most likely reason for its inclusion in the tale. On the other hand, the origin of the tale itself could well have preceded the advent of Christianity given its shamanic aspects.

Now it so happens that the king of the land the youngest son journeys to has a daughter, a maiden queen, "who has made a proclamation that she will wed him that can hide himself from her". However "no man can hide himself from her, and all these men has she slain, for he that cannot hide himself from her is cast down from the top of the castle". With the assistance of his animal helpers, the youngest son succeeds in hiding himself from the queen though, and the story ends happily with a great feast to celebrate the union of the two young people.

One of the attributes often credited to shamans, as well as to witches and other kinds of magical practitioner, is the ability to communicate with the animals, and the youngest son clearly has this in the story. Another attribute of shamans is they have helpers in other realities and the three animals the youngest son encounters on his journey fulfill this role.

The story can be regarded as shamanic in other respects too. For example, the young man goes through the process of an initiation during the course of the tale in the same way as an apprentice shaman would.

The term "initiation" can be used to denote a body of rites and oral teachings whose purpose is to produce a decisive alteration in the religious and social status of the person to be initiated. In philosophical terms, initiation is equivalent to a basic change in existential condition; the novice emerges from his ordeal endowed with a totally different being from that which he possessed before his initiation; he has become another (Eliade, 1958, p.x).

On the other hand, the inclusion of the fish in this tale is probably a reference to *The Book of Tobit*, a book of scripture that is part of the Catholic and Orthodox biblical canon. In it Tobias (Tobit's son) is attacked by a giant fish, whose heart, liver and gall bladder are removed to make medicines. The angel Raphael, sent by God to heal Tobit and to free Sarah from the demon of lust Ashmodai, then instructs Tobias to use the fish's gall to cure Tobit's (his father's) blindness.

So how is it that a tale which clearly has pagan roots includes such references to Christianity? The answer is of course that over time all folktales tend to get modified as they are handed down.

Our ancestors traveled around narrating, singing, or acting

out the stories handed down through the ages. Obviously the plots and characters and locations adopted different meanings as they traversed the landscapes and cultures of the planet; they took on regional variations which changed through time, both "accidentally", by a kind of "Chinese whisper" process, and through deliberate manipulation for propaganda purposes (Ford, 2008, p.37).

There is, however, another reason or the apparent mixed messages. In Georgia, as was the case all through the region, "The lines between being obviously Christian or obviously Muslim could be indistinct. In the Caucasus people in both religious categories enjoyed alcohol, were far removed from clerical authority, and practiced a form of folk religion that bore only scant resemblance to the orthodox varieties found elsewhere" (King, 2008, p.56). Although this particular quote refers to the past, by and large the same situation still applies today, especially in the more remote and inaccessible areas.

Bibliography

Booker, C. (2004) *The Seven Basic Plots*: *Why we tell Stories*, London: Continuum.

Eliade, M. (2003) *Rites and Symbols of Initiation*, Putnam, Connecticut: Spring Publications (originally published by Harper Bros., New York, 1958).

Ford, J. (2008) *Never Point at a Rainbow*, Newtown, Powys: Superscript Books.

King, C. (2008) *The Ghost of Freedom*, New York: Oxford University Press Inc.

Wardrop, M. (1894) *Georgian Folk Tales*, London: David Nutt

The Bat'onebi: The Spirits Who Live Beyond the Black Sea

The *bat'onebi* are spirits who are believed to live beyond the Black Sea and they are sent out by their superior in all directions, in order to test the loyalty of mankind. During the daytime, the *bat'onebi* move about on mules. In the evening, however, they return to the houses of the sick and reside in the bodies of the stricken. *Bat'onebi* are to be obeyed without question, as resistance only enrages them. Nonetheless, their hearts can be conquered with tenderness and caresses; thus, it is possible to protect oneself from calamity. They are said to enjoy gentle songs and the bright sound of instrumental music.

The blisters from chickenpox (*q'vavili*, literally: flowers) and the redness from measles (*ts'itela*, literally: redness) are said to be signs of the arrival of the *bat'onebi*. As a rule, such infectious diseases, called "the Lords" (*bat'onebi*), or "the Angels" (*angelozebi*), "visited" a person once in a lifetime only, and therefore contracting such a disease was regarded as a sacred duty, a service to God. The people believed that some supernatural creatures, which appeared in the house, caused such diseases.

To cure the patient and keep his or her relatives from danger, it was necessary to please "the Lords" in every way possible, to make them feel good. For this it was considered helpful to use bright colored fabrics and clothes, to keep away from strong and unpleasant odors, and also from sharp objects. The patient's relatives were not allowed to smoke, to drink alcohol, to slaughter animals, to shoot, even to speak in a loud voice and to quarrel. The people entertained "the Lords" with special songs and dances; they laid "the Lords' table" with ritual food and erected "the Lords' tree" decorated with viands and bright ribbons. When the patient was cured, the ceremony of "seeing-off the Lords" was held.

When *bat'onebi* came, it was also thought reasonable to pray for help to St. Barbara, to St. John the Baptist, and to St. Queen Tamara. Other efficient means of cure included a vow to take a sacrificial animal to the church, or to perform a ritual.

In preparation for the ritual, the patient's bed and room would be decorated with colorful fabrics and flowers. Visitors would wear red or white garments and walk around the sick person with presents for the *bat'onebi* in their hands. A table full of sweets and a kind of Christmas tree would be prepared for them too. If the illness became worse, the family of the patient would turn to the ritual of "asking-for-pardon" (*sabodisho*) and a *mebodishe* (a woman who has access to the *bat'onebi* and acts as a mediator) would be invited to contact them to find out what they want and to win them over. Once the patient recovered, the *bat'onebi* would then be escorted on their way, back to where they came from.

Even today practitioners can be found who work with the *bat'onebi*, and the following article is about one such person:

Exorcist From Gali

By **Nana Abshilava**

Brosse Street Journal

Wednesday, December 7 2005

"Otche nash, eje isi na nebesi, da svyatitsa imya tvoio, da budet carstvo tvoio.... Amin, Amin, Amin."

It's the 23rd Psalm in Russian, offered up as a prayer by Iliko Rostobaya - on a mobile phone.

"I don't have right to give you an interview," he says. "I am a savior of people and I do what the God and angels tell me. They are my journalists, and it is enough."

Rostobaya is about 60 years old. He lives in Perigali (first village of Gali), in an area that the disputed Georgia once controlled before losing it to the unrecognized government of Abkhazia after a bloody civil war 14 years ago. He serves his God and cures people afflicted by batonebi (demons). Some local people call him Ilia III. (Ilia II is the Patriarch of the Georgian Orthodox Church.)

Before the war, Rostobaya was the director of the house of culture in nearby Achigvara for over 30 years. He has a wife, two sons and one daughter. He suffered from obesity for many years and at one time weighed about 150 kg (330 pounds). He traveled to several countries looking for help, without success. In Germany they tried forcing him to drink so much cold water he couldn't eat. He also tried acupuncture. But he says he cured himself. He suffered bad dreams that tortured him until he says "batonebi" came to him. He then lost 80 kg (about 175 pounds).

There are said to be 12 types of batonebi, and each causes a different illness. The word "batonebi" in the Georgian language can be used either as the plural form for gentleman, or it can be translated as "Lord." But in Abkhazia and the neighboring Georgian province of Mingrelia, "batonebi" can sometimes mean "demon".

"I always had dreams where two men pushed me to commit suicide, and nobody could help me," Rostobaya said. "And when I awoke I wanted to kill myself. It continued for many years. Then I began to feel that I was a savior and I could cure people from batonebi."

"Before I began God's service, I was like other people. I loved women. I worked."

"Batonebi can curve a person's body. When it happens, the person doesn't understand what he does. He can kill anybody, even his child, because the devil lives in his body. But I can help them, because I am a savior. I am God's messenger. Batonebi appears because of sins which people do."

Another batonebi is blamed for the red body rash also known as German measles. According to Rostobaya, when you have the disease, you can forecast the future or predict when others will catch the disease.

He says that if people get a big batonebi, they can't bathe for 40 days, can't go into mourning, can't drink alcohol, and can't wash and iron clothes. He says their body will curve and they may even try to crawl under a sofa.

He says such ill people need comfort, music, song and dance - and their own savior. The savior plays a panduri (Georgian folk music instrument) and sings, prays and lights candles. Patients who come from afar live in his house.

Nobody knows where the batonebi legend began, and why it is known only in Abkhazia and Mingrelia. Medical workers are sceptical.

"When children are small, parents must bring them to doctors and inoculate them against redness and pockmarks," said Maya Abakelia, a pediatrician. "I think (batonebi believers) are neurotics; I think they go mad."

The Georgian Orthodox Church doesn't recognize batonebi and its Saviors.

"I don't believe Iliko. Demons can be cured and only by the church. I also had such patients, and we followed rules. I was starving for them for 40 days and praying, no song and dance like they do. I don't give them permission to come to church with a panduri . This is a temple and not a concert hall," said Father Sergei, priest of the Ilori temple in nearby Ochamchira.

"I cure a lot of diseases," Rostobaya said. "For example, I cured a couple from Gali with AIDS. I cured a lot of people from every country. I am famous. Everybody knows me. I cure over the phone. My words cure them even over the mobile. Even my saliva helps them.

"I had a guest from Russia two months ago. She will have an accident tomorrow," said Iliko as he shows a photo of a young girl. "She is a reporter like you, but if I don't help her, she'll die."

Helped by a dream, he found an old church that was buried under 10 meters of earth. Helped by his son and some neighbors, he dug it up and found old bones, axes and other weapons.

Some people believe it is the burial spot of Queen Tamar Bagrationi. They built a big cross that lights up every night to mark the spot.

"When archaeologists from Tbilisi heard about the church, they came and wanted to make an examination to see in what century it was built," Rostobaya said. "But I didn't allow them, because (the batonebi) don't give me the right."

He dreams about rebuilding the church. But for now, after each recovery from a batonebi, he and his patients perform an animal sacrifice at the church he found.

It has been suggested by Professor Paul Badham that "The main reason for studying religious experience is that it has so often been foundational for religion. Most people who believe in God do so because they have had experiences which make them think that God is real" (in 'The Case for Studying Religious Experience across Cultures and Traditions', BASR Bulletin No.112 May 2008). However, perhaps rather than religious experience being foundational for most people who believe in God or the power of the spirits, it might be more accurate to say that what it actually does is to reinforce their belief at various points in their lives. And perhaps Rostobaya's convictions, as expressed in the article above, can best be understood in this light.

It should perhaps be pointed out that this account has not been presented here to prove or disprove the power of shamanism. The reason for offering it to you is rather to show what a crucial role the pagan religious practitioner or the shaman still has to play, even in the lives of people in the 21st century, and how the role has evolved to suit the times we are now living in – "My words cure them even over the mobile".

It is generally agreed that part of the healing process is being able to put a name to whatever condition a patient is suffering from, and that naming an inauspicious condition is halfway to removing it. Embodying the invisible in a tangible symbol, such as that of the bat'onebi, can be regarded as a big step towards remedying it and, as Turner (1995) points out, is not so far removed from the practice of the modern psychoanalyst. Once something is grasped by the mind, it can then be dealt with and mastered. Thus the goal of therapy is not only to cure but also to give meaning to sickness. However, it has been suggested that something else is required first before the healing process can take effect because "not only must the disease be named, but the diagnosis must reflect the shared world view of healer and client to be effective" (Villoldo & Krippner, 1987, p.193). This is because when the world view of the practitioner is not shared by the client, then the client clearly has less reason to be as committed to the process as he/she might otherwise be, and his/her expectation of recovery will be adversely affected too.

On the other hand, not everyone would necessarily agree with Villoldo and Krippner. It has been suggested that "By performing a liturgical order the participants accept, and indicate to themselves and to others that they accept whatever is encoded in the canon of that order" (Rappaport, 1999, p.119) provided, of course, they are not acting. Though acceptance can be regarded as intrinsic to liturgical performance it should not be confused with belief. For acceptance is a public act whereas belief is a private state (see Rappaport, 1999, pp.119-120). In that case, we need to ask whether acceptance is really enough or if belief is required too in order to gain the maximum possible benefit from the sort of rituals we are considering here. In view of the fact that sometimes rituals take place to cure patients who are unaware of the fact that they are even being treated, in cases of distant healing or when someone is in a coma, it would seem that neither acceptance nor belief is necessarily required on the part of the patient in order for the process to be effective – and that what is required in effect is a miracle for what happens cannot really be explained any other way.

A translation of the lyrics to one of the many songs about the bat'onebi is presented below. *Laynany* was collected in 1987 at *Akhalsopeli* (a district of *Qvareli*) by members of *Ensemble Mzetamze*, an ensemble of ethnomusicologists dedicated exclusively to the musical traditions of Georgian women and from whom information on this folk custom was obtained, and the lyrics were translated by Ketevan Kalandadze:

Iavnana, vardos Nana, Iavnanina,
Nana da Nana, vardo (my rose), *Nana, Iavnanina.*
We are seven sisters and brothers, *Iavnanina.*
We traveled through seven villages, *Iavnanina.*
We entered the villages so quietly, *Iavnanina*
that not even a single dog barked, *Iavnanina.*

We entered the yard so quietly, *Iavnanina,*
And got into the beds of the ill, *Iavnanina,*
So that the mother did not notice, *Iavnanina,*
Nobody noticed, *Iavnaina.*
I picked violets and made a bouquet of roses, *Iavnanina.*
I spread them over our ill ones, *Iavnanina.*
Iavnana, Vardos Nana, Iavnanina.

Bibliography

Badham, P. (2008) 'The Case for Studying Religious Experience across Cultures and Traditions', in BASR Bulletin No.112.

Rappaport, R.A. (1999) *Ritual and Religion in the Making of Humanity*, Cambridge: Cambridge University Press.

Turner, V. (1995) *The Ritual Process: Structure and Anti-Structure*, Chicago, Illinois: Aldine Publishing Company (first published in 1969).

Villoldo, A., & Krippner, S. (1987) *Healing States: A Journey into the World of Spiritual Healing and Shamanism*, New York: Fireside.

The Pomegranate Stream

The pomegranate tree has been cultivated in the Caucasus since ancient times and plays an important part in Georgian cuisine too, so it is therefore not surprising that it features prominently in this tale.

In Judaism the pomegranate is a symbol for righteousness, because it is said to have 613 seeds which corresponds with the 613 *mitzvot* or commandments of the Torah. Some Jewish scholars even believe that it may well have been the forbidden fruit of the Garden of Eden, which was not the apple despite the common misconception. Pomegranate is also one of the Seven Species (Hebrew: סינימה תעבש, *Shiv'at Ha-Minim*), the types of fruits and grains enumerated in the Hebrew Bible (Deuteronomy 8:8) as being special products of the Land of Israel.

In the Christian tradition, pomegranates figure in many religious paintings, often in the hands of the Virgin Mary or the Infant Jesus. The fruit, broken or bursting open, is a symbol of the fullness of his suffering and resurrection. And in the Eastern Orthodox Church, pomegranate seeds may be used in *kolyva*, a dish prepared for memorial services as a symbol of the sweetness of the heavenly kingdom. The pomegranate features in the Qur'an too, where it is found growing in the gardens of paradise (55:068).

The pomegranate also has an important part to play in Greek mythology. Persephone is said to have been kidnapped by Hades and was then taken off to live in the underworld as his wife. Her mother, Demeter (goddess of the Harvest), went into mourning for her lost daughter and thus all green things ceased to grow. Zeus, the highest ranking of the Greek gods, could not leave the Earth to die, so he commanded Hades to return Persephone. It was the rule of the Fates that anyone who consumed food or drink in the Underworld was doomed to spend eternity there.

Persephone had no food, but Hades tricked her into eating four pomegranate seeds while she was still his prisoner and so, because of this, she was condemned to spend four months in the Underworld every year. During these four months, when Persephone is sitting on the throne of the Underworld next to her husband Hades, her mother Demeter mourns and no longer gives fertility to the earth. This became an ancient Greek explanation for the seasons.

Even in Greece today, when one buys a new home, it is conventional for a house guest to bring as a first gift a pomegranate, which is placed under/near the *ikonostasi* (home altar) of the house, as a symbol of abundance, fertility and good luck. It is also still customary to break a pomegranate on the ground at weddings and on New Years.

And in Armenia, which borders Georgia, the pomegranate represents fertility, abundance and marriage (adapted from http://en.wikipedia.org/wiki/Pomegranate [accessed 12/12/08]).

Pomegranates were supposed to have sprung from the blood of Dionysus, as anemones from the blood of Adonis, and

violets from the blood of Attis: hence women refrained from eating seeds of pomegranates at the festival of Thesmophoria (Frazer, 1922, p.389).

In *The Pomegranate Stream*, the stream consists of the tears of the king's wife, the mzetu-nakhavi, who is being held captive by the Dev. With the tree submerged under water, it is unable to thrive as it normally would, and the same applies to the king and his kingdom until the queen can be released.

In other words, the fertility and abundance that the pomegranate promises have been put on hold, and can only return to the kingdom when the queen is reunited with the king once again.

The style of storytelling most frequently employed in both fairy tales and in shamanic stories is that of magic realism, in which although "the point of departure is 'realistic' (recognizable events in chronological succession, everyday atmosphere, verisimilitude, characters with more or less predictable psychological reactions), ... soon strange discontinuities or gaps appear in the 'normal', true-to-life texture of the narrative" (Calinescu, 1978, p.386). In other words, what happens is that our expectations based on our intuitive knowledge of physics are ultimately breached and knocked out. In *The Pomegranate Stream*, this point is reached when we are introduced to the man with millstones tied to his knees, running after rabbits.

Rusudan Choloq'ashvili (author of the 2004 publication *Imagery and Beliefs in Georgian Folk Tales* and a Professor of Philology at Tbilisi State University) refers to three types of folktale that can be found in the Georgian tradition – animal tales, fairy tales, and what she refers to as "novelistic" tales. "A character of an animal tale fights to get some food; a character of a fairy tale fights to find a fiancée; and a character of a novelistic tale strives for a tremendous property" (Choloq'ashvili, 2004, p.183). Our tale would seem to fit into the third of these categories, though our hero finds a fiancée in the process too. She goes on to add that "In spite of the differences between these sub-genres, on the whole they have a common plot: the hero goes to get a marvelous thing, overcomes obstacles three times, gets the desired thing and returns as a winner" (Choloq'ashvili, 2004, p.189).

Another observation Choloq'ashvili makes is that "It is inconceivable to end a fairy tale with the death of the hero" (Choloq'ashvili, 2004, p.187), and our tale follows standard practice in this respect. It is also pointed out that in such tales "we [generally] observe rewarding of a customs keeper, as well as punishment of a customs infringer" (Choloq'ashvili, 2004, p.187), and this applies to our tale too.

"For the shaman ... nature's wilderness is the locus for the elicitation of the individual's inner wilderness ... and it is only here that the inner voices awaken into song. The inanimate sermon of pristine deserts, mountains, high plains, and forests instructs from a place beyond idea concept or construct" (Halifax, 1991, p.6). In other words, it is only when the younger son leaves home and sets out on his quest through unknown territory that the inner voices come into play, and the journey he embarks on can in fact be interpreted as an inner journey. The process can be said to commence after the two sons cross nine mountains, and the younger son chooses the right fork.

As for the confusion over the distance traveled, "After they walked a short distance or after they walked a long distance", this is a stylistic device often found in Georgian folktales. It serves the purpose of conveying to us how removed the setting of the tale is from this reality, and to help bring about the severance from the everyday world that it is necessary before Sacred Space, in this case a cave in a mountain, can be entered. Temporal dislocation and "the alteration or the transmutation of space" (Eliade, 1981, p.10) are themes that appear over and over again in shamanic stories and *The Pomegranate Stream* is no exception to the rule.

The symbol of a Mountain, a Tree or a Column situated at the Centre of the World is extremely widely distributed. We may recall the Mount Meru of Indian tradition, Haraberezaita of the Iranians, the Norse Himinbjorg, the "Mount of the Lands" in the Mesopotamian tradition, Mount Tabor in Palestine (which may signify *tabbur* – that is, "navel" or *omphalos*), Mount Gerizim, again in Palestine, which is expressly named the "navel of the earth", and the Golgotha which, for Christians, represented the center of the world etc. (Eliade,

1991, p.42).

Eliade also points out that "In cultures that have the conception of three cosmic regions – those of Heaven, Earth and Hell – the 'centre' constitutes the point of intersection of those regions. It is here that the break-through on to another plane is possible and, at the same time, communication between the three regions" (Eliade, 1991, p.40). The mountain in our story can be seen to represent just such a place, and is a symbol traditionally used for such a purpose. Consider the story of Moses, for example, in the Old Testament, who climbed Mount Sinai to receive God's teachings.

As for the occupant of the cave, a Dev or Devi, this being is an evil giant often found in folktales from the Caucasus.

> With horns and wicked appearance, the devis often had multiple heads that regenerated if severed. Devis lived in [the] underworld or remote mountains, where they hoarded treasures and kept captives. Georgian mythos usually depicted a family of devis, with nine brothers being the average number. Baq'baq'-Devi was most often the strongest and most powerful of the devis. Heroes, generally, had to deceive them with various tricks or games. (Taken from http://rustaveli.tripod.com/mythology.html [accessed 8/12/08]).

The observation is made by the translator D.G. Hunt in the Introduction to *Georgian Folk Tales* that "Whilst a written, "literary" novel or short story might devote paragraphs to descriptions of people or places, these tales usually settle for an adjective or two" (in Dolidze, 1999, p.8). This would seem to be a feature of shamanic stories in general and can also be found in other examples of the genre.

Another point he makes that also applies to *The Pomegranate Stream* is that "Generally speaking, these tales are packed with action. Whilst a written, 'literary' novel or short story might devote paragraphs to descriptions of people or places, these tales usually settle for an adjective or two; 'a thick impassable forest', 'a handsome stately man', or a formula such as the 'not-seen-beneath-the-sun beauty'" (Dolidze, 1999, p.8).

According to the folklorist Rusudan Choloq'ashvili (2006):

> Any given object which appears in a fairy tale may prove to be magical and wondrous. In Georgian fairy tales featuring animals, the most ancient magical objects are: horse-hair, fur, skin, teeth, wings, feathers, horn, heart and liver, and eggs. Also included are objects made from wool (carpets and caps), and implements used on animals (such as whips). The specific characteristics of magical items of animal origin are conditioned by their genetic association with the supernatural beings of which they are a part, and the wondrous powers of which they possess. By means of these magical implements the chief protagonist of fairy tales manages to share the powers of supernatural animals, and thereby obtains their omnipotence, invincibility and fantastical success.

In this particular tale, however, we are not dealing with magical items of animal origin, but with magical items of plant origin, namely the knotgrass and the clover leaf. And it would presumably be the rarity of the four leaf clover that imbues it with its magical qualities. As for the knotgrass, once it established itself in a garden, it is nearly impossible to eradicate, and this accounts for its invincibility and success as a species – qualities it imbues whoever touches it with, in this particular case the frog.

The Pomegranate Stream

There was and there was, what can be better than God, there was a king who had two very good (everyone can wish for sons like that) sons, He had a very great kingdom too, so much so that you would have thought that a dog would not bark at his fortune, but nobody ever saw him smiling. When his sons became adults they went to him and asked:

"Why is it, father, that we have never seen a smile on your face?"

The king replied to them with great sorrow:

"My sons, how can I smile when your beautiful mother was taken away from me by a dev and I haven't heard anything from her since, and I don't even know where she is."

The sons said:

"Let us go and find our mother!"

The king was very happy about that. He called for his army to accompany his sons and they set off together. The sons crossed nine mountains and came to a fork in the road where it divided into two. The road on the right was full of thorns and the road on the left was full of roses and violets. The older son said to the younger:

"There are only two ways here and our mother can only be this side or that side. Let's play heads and tails and choose which roads to take that way. Then we can divide the army too."

They agreed. The youngest son got the road on the right (the one with the thorns). When they decided to divide the army, nobody wanted to go with the younger brother. Only one man did, and he came out and said:

"My mother breastfed you, I am your nanny's son, and I'm not going to leave you, in trouble or in happiness."

The oldest son took the whole army and went on the road with roses and violets. The younger son went on the thorny road, and he only had his nanny's son to accompany him. They walked the whole day until they came to a field. There they saw a man who had millstones tied to his knees, and that way he was running after rabbits, trying to catch them. The travelers were very surprised at this, and so they asked him:

"Are you crazy or what? What are you doing? Why do you make your work harder with these heavy millstones on your knees?"

The hunter answered:

"If I don't do that and run after the rabbits, I'm much faster than them, and I'll be running too fast to catch them. So only with the help of these millstones can I catch them."

The travelers were very surprised and so they asked:

"Where are you from "So Fast"? What country? And is everyone like you there? Or is it only you?"

"It is only me," he said. "The rest of the people walk the same way as you do. I learned how to do it with the help of a talisman. If you give me your bows and arrows, I can take you inside the hole where I learned it, and then you can learn to run this fast in 24 hours too."

The travelers gave him their bows and arrows, but only the nanny's son went into the hole with the hunter, while the king's son waited outside for him. After 24 hours the nanny's son came out of the hole and said:

"I have learned it now."

They went walking again and, after crossing another nine mountains, they came to a field and saw a man lying on his stomach on the ground and laughing. The travelers were very surprised at this too, and so they asked him:

"Why are you laughing?"

"Because it's very funny! Down in the earth the ants have a nest. There are too many of them and not enough space for everyone so they are trying to divide what they have and arguing over it."

Once again the travelers were very surprised and so they asked:

"Who are you? Where do you come from? How can you see that far? Can everyone see like you in the country where you come from or are you the only one?"

"I'm the only one," he answered. "I learned how to do it with the help of a talisman. If you give me your shields, I can take you inside the hole where I learned it, and you can learn to see this far in 24 hours too."

"We don't have our swords and what do we need these shields for in any case?" said the travelers, and so they agreed.

The nanny's son went into the hole while the king's son waited outside for a day and a night. When he came out of the hole the sun was already shining.

The king's son told his servant:

"You see we don't have any swords and shields, and if you have learnt anything we can find out now. Look to all four sides and let me know if you can see anything."

The nanny's son covered his eyes with his hands, looked in three directions and said nothing. Then he looked south and shouted:

"Under the high bare mountain I can see a very beautiful pomegranate tree growing, and a stream is flowing over it. There's a cave and king's palace in that mountain too. A Mzetunakhavi (a woman of outstanding beauty) is sitting on a golden throne on her own and she's weeping bitterly. The cave hasn't got a door. As quick as a wink the cave opens up and closes again. Only wind can get in."

"But you're that quick now," the king's son said, "you can go in and take me with you!

And so they went there together. After they walked a short distance or after they walked a long distance, they came to the place. When the cave opened, the nanny's son ran into it, secured the opening with a wedge, and this way let the king's son in too.

The Mzetunakhavi was very surprised and asked them:

"Who are you? Where do you come from? The Dev who lives here is so fierce that even birds don't dare to fly in the sky here and ants don't dare to crawl on the earth. Go away and save yourselves. For the time being, he's gone hunting, but if he sees you both on his return he'll kill all three of us."

The king's son told her his story. The Mzetunakhavi shouted, hugged him very hard and said:

"You are my son, so please go away and save yourself – go now, this very minute, before it's too late!"

She started to cry bitterly and her tears filled the water pipes and started to flow down over the pomegranate tree. And that was how they came to realize that the pomegranate stream was the tears of Mzetunakhavi that had gathered in the pipes. The king's son said to the nanny's son:

"Look and find out for us if Dev is near or still far away."

The nanny's son looked and said:

"He's behind the nine mountains. He killed a deer and has hung it on a tree. His shield is on the ground and now he's trying to skin the deer, and he's not even half way through yet."

Then he looked around and, in the corner of the cave, he found a small golden box, decorated with pearls and precious stones. The box did not have a lid, and it did not have a lock or a key either.

"How can a beautiful bird be placed in a box like this?" he asked, surprised.

"This bird is the Dev's soul," said the Mzetunakhavi, "and nobody can harm him as long as this bird is safe."

"How does the Dev himself open the box?"

"With Amirani's key."

"What's Amirani's key?"

"The clover," said the Mzetunakhavi. "Amirani was chained to the mountain for a very long time. The earth, sky and every living being felt sorry for him but nobody could help. His chain was unbreakable. One day an ant went to Amirani and said to him: 'I feel very sorry for you and if you would be grateful then I could help to set you free.' Amirani laughed and said: 'On this earth there is nothing smaller than you, but it seems you have the bravest heart and want to do the impossible.' The ant said: 'Now I will tell you something and you must listen. Once a snake caught a frog and wanted to swallow it. A hawk then attacked the snake and the frog managed to escape. The badly hurt frog then found a piece of knotgrass (*Polygonum aviculare*), rubbed his legs on it, and all his injuries just disappeared. He was restored to perfect health again. I was astonished, went over to the knotgrass and praised it. The knotgrass said to me: 'I am nothing compared to the clover, which can break any lock or chain. You only need to touch the object you want to break open with it.' When I heard that, I crawled over to the clover, cut off its fourth leaf, and took it with me.' The ant crawled over to Amirani, touched the chain with the clover leaf, and the chain immediately fell apart. Amirani set himself free and blessed the ant: 'In future, because of this good deed you've done, you will be able to carry objects one thousand times bigger than your own body, with no trouble at all.' Amirani was free so he threw away the leaf. Unfortunately, this very same Dev found it, and ever since then, he has kept it somewhere.

The nanny's son looked around and inside one of the walls he saw Amirani's key. He removed it, touched the box with it, the box opened, and he took out the bird and gave it to the king's son saying:

"Hold it tightly and make sure you don't let it fly away."

The king's son held the bird as tightly as he could and asked the nanny's son:

"Can you look at the Dev to see what he's doing now?"

"May your enemy always be in the situation he is now – because he cannot even hold a knife in his hand. He's dropped it and he can't breathe."

The King's son tore the head off the bird.

"What's he doing now?"

His head has come off his shoulders and he's dropped down dead.

The Mzetunakhavi laughed and said that they had been saved. They all became very cheerful. They collected some gold and precious stones and left the Dev's castle once and for all. Then they walked a short way or a long way, they crossed the nine mountains and came to the junction where two brothers had originally separated and had each gone their own way. There they met the older son with his army and told him their story. The older son took the Mzetunakhavi hostage, and made all the soldiers in his army promise to keep what he had done a secret. He even had the audacity to threaten his own mother:

"See this army? If you tell what happened to anybody or to the king, then they'll kill you and the king."

The Mzetunakhavi was very scared. The older son sent a messenger to his father saying: "I've defeated the Devs in their country with my army, I destroyed their castles, took their wealth, and I am bringing my mother home with me."

The king was over the moon, and all the people in his kingdom were delighted when they heard the news too. The older son and his army were met with music and great festivity. The king sat his son on his own throne and then proclaimed:

"Everyone in my kingdom come and pay your respects to the hero!"

Big or little, they all came to congratulate the older brother on the victory, bow down in front of him, and kiss his knees. As for the younger brother and the nanny's son, after some time they arrived home too, exhausted and with all their clothes torn - without their bows, arrows or their shields. They came and said:

"We were the ones who saved the queen. So why are you now behaving this way? The person you're bowing down to did nothing!"

Everyone was surprised and laughed when they heard this. Some of them said: "They must be crazy", some said: "They've got no consciences", and others said "They're liars". Nobody believed them.

The king was furious and said this about his young son:

"He's jealous of his brother and that must be why he says that. Kick this useless good-for-nothing out of my palace and put him in the pen with the geese."

The queen was very disturbed by this, but she was too scared to say a word. And the younger son was so upset that he had a heart attack and died shortly after. Nobody even acknowledged his death but the queen could not stay silent any more, and she started crying in front of the king. The king wanted to know why – what had upset her so much.

"It's bad if I say it and it's bad if I don't!" shouted the queen. "If I don't say it then it won't be right in the eyes of God, and if I say it then it means we'll both lose our lives."

But the king insisted on an answer in any case:

"If you don't tell me the secret, I'll kill you and kill myself, too," he said.

Then the queen told her husband everything, and the king instantly regretted the way he had behaved. He called for everyone from his kingdom to assemble and they buried his son with full honors. At the side of his grave he built a marble castle to commemorate him, and ordered that at certain fixed times, at dawn and sunset, everyone should go to this castle to pay their respects. Everyone obeyed the king's order and every day at the appointed times, people went there to pay their respects. After all, nobody could disobey the king – it was more than their lives were worth! But a strange thing was happening exactly at those times, for every day, a cock sat on top of the castle and cried cock a doodle do. The king was informed about that.

This must be some sign. There must be a reason why the cock comes every day. Go and find someone who understands the language of the animals and bring them to me.

The nanny's son said:

"I know the language of the animals, my king. That cock talks about the ungratefulness on this earth. When your son was alive you caged him in a pen, and when he's dead he is placed in a marble castle. When he was alive he was judged unjustly, and now he's dead you worship him. What help is that for the poor soul!"

The king was ashamed, thought for a while, and then said:

"Nothing will come out of this cock's behavior either. If he knew that much, then why didn't he shout earlier? What help is it dead or alive? Shoot an arrow at the bird and kill him."

The king's archers went to kill the cock, but the cock opened his wings and flew away across nine mountains. The king was left both speechless and chastened.

I left my troubles there and brought joy here.

(Taken from Virsaladze, E., 1984, *Folktales of the World: Georgian Folktales*, Tbilisi: Nakaduli Publishing).

Soul loss is the term used to describe the way parts of the psyche become detached when we are faced with traumatic situations, which is perhaps what can be said to happen to the younger son when he comes under threat. In psychological terms, it is known as dissociation and it works as a defense mechanism, a means of displacing unpleasant feelings, impulses or thoughts into the unconscious. In shamanic terms, these split off parts can be found in non-ordinary reality, "across nine mountains" in this particular tale, and are only accessible to those familiar with its topography, in other words the geography of non-ordinary reality and how to locate spirits and places there. Soul retrieval entails the shaman journeying to find the missing parts and then returning them to the client seeking help. The shaman, in the words of Eliade, "is the great specialist in the human soul: he alone 'sees' it, for he knows its 'form' and its destiny" (Eliade, 1989, p.8).

There are some who believe that "The soul, the locus of one's personal identity and characterized by mental functions like memory, allows the individual person to survive bodily corruption, remember its past life, and possibly even perceive its own unique world through such abilities as mental telepathy" (Price, 1996, p.419). There are others, however, who believe that the very idea of life after death, in a psychological rather than a physiological or biochemical sense, is unintelligible.

But why should it not be possible to suppose experiences can occur after death that are linked with experiences had before death, with our personal identities remaining intact? And this could well be what happens to the younger son in our story when he shape-shifts into the body of the cock.

The problem is we can only be said to have experiences at all if we are aware of some form of world so the idea of survival in some form is dependent on there being another world or reality. Some see this other reality as a kind of dream-world, one of mental images, which is how the world a shaman experiences when he journeys might be described by an "outsider".

However, "there is nothing imaginary about a mental image. It is an actual entity, as real as anything can be" (Price, 1996, p.422). Moreover, for those who experience it "an image world would be just as 'real' as this present world is" (Price, 1996, p.423). If we can accept this proposition, then the journey undertaken by the shaman for the purpose of soul recovery or retrieval, and the way he/she describes the experience in the shamanic story, becomes much easier to comprehend. In the case of the younger son, however, there is no soul retrieval, and the story ends with him being apparently lost to this reality forever.

Among people who once believed in shamanism but were later converted to various world religions, former shamanism may be revealed through an analysis of their folklore and folk beliefs, and this can be applied to Georgia. Georgians have officially lived under the ideological influence of Christianity since the fifth century and then, more recently, under the influence of Communism, during which time pagan rites were frowned upon and their practitioners persecuted. Therefore it is hardly surprising few have been able to survive, and those that have tend to be found in the inaccessible mountainous regions. This enables doubters today to say the findings and data are insufficient to show that shamanism even existed in Georgia. However, folk tales such as *The Pomegranate Stream*, and the folk customs still practiced today, even by the more sophisticated urbanites, would seem to indicate otherwise.

Bibliography

Calinescu, M. (1978) 'The Disguises of Miracle: Notes on Mircea Eliade's Fiction.' In Bryan Rennie (ed.) (2006) *Mircea Eliade: A Critical Reader*, London: Equinox Publishing Ltd.

Choloq'ashvili, R. (2004) Imagery and Beliefs in Georgian Folk Tales, Tbilisi: Nekeri.

Choloqashvili R. (2006) Magical objects in Georgian fairy tales featuring animals (Summary). In *Amirani* Vol. 14-15. 2006. PDF (taken from http://www.caucasology.com/amirani.htm [accessed 10/12/08]).

Dolidze, N.I. (1999) *Georgian Folk Tales*, Tbilisi: Merani Publishing House.

Eliade, M. (1989) *Shamanism: Archaic techniques of ecstasy*, London: Arkana (first published in the USA by Pantheon Books 1964).

Eliade, M. (1991) *Images and Symbols*, New Jersey: Princeton University Press (The original edition is copyright Librairie Gallimard 1952).

Halifax, J. (1991) *Shamanic Voices*, London: Arkana (first published in 1979).

Price, H.H. (1996) 'The Soul Survives and Functions after Death.' In Michael Peterson, William Hasker, Bruce Reichenbach, and David Basinger (eds.) *Philosophy of Religion: Selected Readings*, New York: Oxford University Press. Pp.447-456.

The Doctor Lukman

The people of Abkhazia live in a mountainous region that is situated on the south eastern coast of the Black Sea. The name the Abkhaz call themselves is *apsua* and their ancient territory they call *Ashvy* (the land of the Abkhaz). As for the Abkhaz language, it belongs to the Abkhazo-Adyghian group of the Caucasian family, and there are two dialects: Abzhui and Bzyb.

According to legend, when God was distributing land to all the different peoples of the earth, the Abkhazians were busy entertaining guests at the time. Because it would have been impolite to leave before their guests, the Abkhazians arrived late, and all that God had left by then was some stones. Out of these it is said he created a land of mountains - hard to grow anything on, but very beautiful.

The first written mention of the Abkhaz people is believed to be the note on the *Abesla* tribes living in Asia Minor, found in the records of the Assyrian ruler Tiglath-pileser. The Proto-Abkhaz tribes Apsil, Misiman, Abazg, and Svanig were known to the ancient Greek and Roman historians like Hekateus of Miletus, Strabo and Flavius Arrianus. In the 1st century AD the Proto-Abkhaz tribes set up their own principalities that were united with the Cazika Principality in the 4th century. The 7th—8th centuries witnessed the consolidation of the Proto-Abkhaz tribes into the Abkhaz nation (taken from *The Peoples of the Red Book* http://www.eki.ee/books/redbook/abkhaz.shtml [accessed 20/10/08]).

Subsequently, the Abkhaz nation was incorporated into Georgia, and then subordinated by Turkey, before eventually becoming a Russian protectorate. After the Crimean and Caucasian wars in the mid-nineteenth century, Abkhaz autonomy became unnecessary for the Russian government, so the last Prince Shervashidze was sent into exile, and tsarist power and Russian bureaucracy were established. In February 1921 the Abkhaz SSR was set up, and in December of that year it was incorporated into the Georgian SSR according to the Union treaty (adapted from The Peoples of the Red Book http://www.eki.ee/books/redbook/abkhaz.shtml [accessed 20/10/08]).

Although the Georgians claim that Abkhazia is an integral part of their territory, after the conflict that broke out in the summer of 2008, the Russians recognized the independence of Abkahzia. As the rest of the world has not followed suit, the current status of the people remains unclear.

Polytheistic rituals and beliefs in Abkhazia are inextricably linked to the structure of the extended family or lineage - in other words, all those who share the same surname. Each lineage has its own sacred place, or *a'nyxa*, and "in the past each lineage had its own protective spirits to whom sacrifices and prayers were made at an annual gathering ... These sacred places are natural locations, high up in the mountains, or in forest groves, by springs or rivers, cliffs or sacred trees" (Rachel Clogg in Hewitt, 1999, p.211). They took the place of a church or a mosque and were places where refuge could be sought.

We know from the writings of Procopius of Caesaria in the sixth century that groves and trees were at one time worshipped by the people. Even today certain trees, groves, and mountains are sacred to clans and villages and are centers of religious gatherings. They embody the strength of a patrilineal line, its connection to a certain place, and to God above. We also know that

In the past, many families worshipped their ancestors, believing that they were linked with an animal, plant, or element of nature, though all that is left of this today is an indication in some Abkhaz surnames that they may derive from the names of animals or plants. The numerous deities traditionally worshipped by the Abkhaz were also almost all associated with the natural world, or certain animals or elements within it. The 'god of gods' in the Abkhaz pantheon is Ants^{w}a, the creator, in whom all the other gods are contained ... The first toast still to be given at feasts is one to Ants^{w}a, in the form of "Ants^{w}a, you give us the warmth of your eyes" (Rachel Clogg in Hewitt, 1999, p.213).

Other gods include Afa, who rules the thunder and other aspects of the weather; Shasta, protector of blacksmiths and all artisans; Azhveipshaa, the spirit of the forest, wild animals, and hunting; and Aitar, the protector of domestic animals.

When it comes to considering the religious beliefs and practices of the people, the paper 'The Shamaness of the Abkhazians' by Andrejs Johansons [translated from the German by *Park McGinty*] taken from *History of Religions*, Vol. 11, No. 3. (Feb., 1972), pp. 251-256, is of particular interest to us as it focuses on the prominent position which was occupied by the shamaness among the Abkhazians.

In Abkhaz, a woman who engaged in prophecy and the art of oracles as well as certain cultic observances was called *acaaju* ("the questioner"). The *acaaju* played an important role in the community and people would travel from far and wide to seek their advice.

... The foremost obligation of the *acaaju* was to ascertain who had caused a specific illness in order to find out the necessary remedies. Sometimes she obtained ecstatic inspiration and cried out the name and the demands of the angered divinity. At other times she went lightly across the room or even sat on a high seat and acted as though she was carrying on a conversation with the divinity, to whom she directed questions and from whom she received answers. After a while, she made known the result. For example, the illness could have been sent by Afy on account of a neglected sacrifice. Another important god from whose wrath the people had to protect themselves was Šesšu (also Šašv or Šašvy-ach-du), the supernatural protector of the smithy or forge. As a rule, this god would grow angry over a false oath which the sick person or some one of his relatives had made in the smithy.

The forge had among the Abkhazians, perhaps to an even greater extent than among several other Caucasian peoples, the character of a cult place. If there was no real forge in the neighborhood, a small "symbolic" one was built in the garden or somewhere in the courtyard and used only for religious purposes.

The Abkhazian blacksmith was not only an artisan, but even more, a representative of Šesšu and the mediator between this god and human beings. He also directed the frequent performances of the oath in Šesšu's name, which were carried out with solemn ceremonies in an exactly prescribed form.

It goes without saying that between the smith and the *acaaju* there was close collaboration. If it was a question of discovering the guilty party who had offended Šesšu with a false oath, the *acaaju* employed not only the methods previously mentioned but also material resources. That is, she spread out beans in front of her, and on the basis of the arrangement of these found out the name of the transgressor. If occasion arose, astrology was also taken into account, thus one more technique of divination in which she had to be skilled.

The divine will being ascertained, the *acaaju* reported what kind of animals were to be brought as expiatory sacrifice. She often carried out the sacrifice herself. Beyond that, she also performed various actions of a magical sort. Thus, for example, she led some domestic animal three times around the sick person, after which it was driven away toward the forest, supposedly carrying the sickness away with it. As payment for her help, the *acaaju* received either the skins of the sacrificial animals and a part of the meat or a rather substantial sum of money.

It is interesting to note that the *acaaju* was called by a masculine name during the prophecy, and that she was generally spoken to as if she were a man. A ritual change of sex of this kind a common accompanying phenomenon of shamanism in many parts of the world, and it can take the form of imitative behavior in which identity with a god or spirit is temporarily supposed to be brought about (adapted from http://www.circassianworld.com/pdf/Shamaness.pdf [accessed 20/10/08]).

Illnesses could be caused by a whole range of factors apart from the wrath of such gods as Afy and Šesšu. For example, lengthy sufferings with fever were considered to be "caused by the water" and in such cases Dzyzlan, the Mistress of the Waters or the Water Mother, was called on for help. And rituals would take place at her place of residence - at a pure sweet water lake or a stream. Another widespread belief was that serious illnesses could be caused by a person entering water the moment when the Rainbow drank from it.

The story that follows is not only about illnesses but also about the person who is said to have been the very first doctor:

Man had hardly appeared in the world, before he began to think how not to die of hunger, how to get warm on a bitterly cold day and how to find medicine against illness. The more people there were, the more illness appeared.

So, around that time, there also appeared a doctor by the name of Lukman. He conceived the idea of relieving the suffering of people, of finding a remedy for illness. Lukman searched for various medicinal herbs and roots in the fields, in the ravines, along banks of rivers and streams, and in mountain pastures. For the healing of wounds he found *akhurbgits* (plantain), for the treatment of Siberian ulcers, *ashkhardan* (a medicinal root), for the relief of malaria, *adjakva* (a winter multi-flowered plant), and he discovered the medicinal properties of a great many other herbs. With flowers, with leaves, with roots he cured people of all kinds of ailments. There was only one that he did not know about: how to cure a toothache.

On one occasion a snake crawled to him and began to beg him, "I frequently have terrible headaches, cure me!" Lukman agreed to help him, but at the same time he asked whether he knew a remedy for toothache. "If it is not possible to soothe the tooth with medicine, then it is necessary to pull it out, since there is nothing worse than this suffering," answered then snake.

"Yes, I understand," said Lukman, "but the trouble is that I do not know with what and how one ought to pull the teeth."

"You can pull a tooth with something similar to my head, with a contraption that would be able to open and close."

"That is good advice. In gratitude for it I will instruct you of the most sure remedy for a headache. As soon as you have a headache, lie down on a highway, rolling yourself into a ball, pressing your head to the ground and closing your eyes. Simply lie motionless, trying to sleep, not paying attention to anything. After about an hour the headache will pass completely."

"Thank you, friend," said the snake, and it crawled into the bushes, in order to instruct all the snakes of the remedy for headaches.

This is why snakes, even today, after rolling themselves into a ball, settle themselves in the middle of the road; and people, creeping up to them, kill them.

On one occasion, Lukman, after pelting rain, wanted to get across a river which was a swollen torrent. The narrow little bridge, thrown across it, was slippery, since the water was coming up through the cracks from below. Lukman slipped and fell into the river. With difficulty he managed to clamber out on to dry ground. Most of the medicines which he was carrying with him were lost, and only a few items were deposited by the current on to the bank. Lukman gathered up the surviving medicines, and with them he cures people even to this day.

The story was taken from Bgazhba, Kh.S. (1985) *Abkhazian Tales,* translated from the Russian, with new Introduction by D.G. Hunt. (Russian edition published by Alashara Publishing House, Sukhumi). The collection can be found in the University College of London library, and it was donated to the library by the translator.

While on the subject of healing and remedies in Abkhazia, it is interesting to note the unusual longevity that is a feature of the region. This would seem to be, by all accounts, a genuine reality, as the area is indeed home to an inordinate number of extremely healthy elders.

The following are excerpts from the book, "Healthy At 100", by John Robbins, 2006, and they have been adapted from (http://fanaticcook.blogspot.com/2007/10/longevity-in-abkhasia.html [accessed 8/2/09]).

Dr. Sula Benet, anthropologist and author of Abkhasians: The Long-Living People of the Caucasus", lists a number of reasons for Abkhasians' remarkable health and longevity. One she highlighted:

"In Abkhasia, a person's status increases with age, and he or she receives ever more privileges with the passing years. ...

Elders who are poor and known only to their families have greater social standing in Abkhasian society than someone who may have become rich and famous but is not yet an elder.

"When one US researcher explained to a group of Abkhasians that in the wealthy United States, old people are sometimes left homeless and hungry, he was met with total disbelief. Nothing he said could overcome their inability to grasp such a reality."

"In Abkhasia, people are esteemed and seen as beautiful in their old age. Silver hair and wrinkles are viewed as signs of wisdom, maturity, and long years of service. ... It would be considered an insult to be told you are "looking young" or that the years have barely changed you. ... When older people lie about their age, they do not give a younger age, as is common in the West. Instead, they exaggerate how old they are, for this gives them greater standing in their culture."

Of course the diet of the people is likely to be one of the factors that accounts for their longevity too. The traditional Abkhasian diet is essentially lacto-vegetarian, with a rare serving of meat, and with one or two glasses a day of a fermented beverage called 'matzoni', made from the milk of goats, cows, or sheep. At all three meals, the people eat their "beloved abista", a cornmeal porridge, always freshly cooked and served warm, and if they get hungry between meals, Abkhasians typically eat fruit in season from their own orchard or garden. With rare exception, vegetables are eaten raw and freshness of food is considered paramount. Nuts play a major role in Abkhasian cuisine and are the primary source of fat in the Abkhasian diet. Abkhasians also consume no sugar, little salt, and almost no butter. Overeating is considered both socially inappropriate and dangerous, and the people eat slowly and chew thoroughly. With the effects of globalization, though, one doubts whether this is likely to remain the case, and it is unfortunately probably only a matter of time before the staple diet consists of fast food heated up in the ubiquitous microwave as it does in so many other places these days.

Bibliography

Benet, S. (1974) *Abkhasians: The Long-Living People of the Caucasus*, London: Thomson Learning.

Bgazhba, Kh.S. (1985) *Abkhazian Tales*, Translated from the Russian, with new Introduction by D.G. Hunt. (Russian edition published by Alashara Publishing House, Sukhumi).

Hewitt, G. (ed.) (1999) *The Abkhasians: A Handbook*, Richmond, Surrey: Curzon Press.

Robbins, J. (2007) *Healthy at 100*, Ballantine Books (Reprint edition).

An Old Guest

An important aspect of Georgian culture, especially the male culture, is respect for the giving of hospitality. Hospitality and generosity towards a guest are still, and always have been, paramount. A guest can do no wrong. There are stories of a guest violating the host's wife, without receiving a complaint while he is still a guest; but of the host accompanying his guest to the borders of his territory, and then killing him as soon as he steps across the boundary (Dolidze, 1999, p.7).

Part of the ritual of hospitality is the meal: dinner or supper. Generally these will be elaborate affairs lasting several hours, with family and friends sitting at a large table, covered with all manner of dishes. During the dinner, many toasts will be proposed, in speeches often lasting for several minutes or more, and large quantities of wine will be drunk. This part of the ritual is conducted by men, who need a good capacity for alcohol. The women will generally eat a normal meal, with a glass or two of wine, but with no obligation to drink more (Dolidze, 1999, p.7).

And this is how the Canadian anthropologist and researcher Kevin Tuite describes the suppers:

> The Georgian *supra* ...can go on all evening into the wee hours of the morning, with each guest consuming several liters of wine. These heroic quantities of alcohol are drunk in accordance with strict rules: the participant in a *supra* must pronounce a toast – to another guest, to Georgia, to the souls of the departed, etc. – before drinking each glass, or drinking horn, of wine. The toasts are frequently occasions for a display of eloquence, and are accompanied by song and recitations of poetry (Tuite, 1995, p.13).

Although to us the lavishness of such entertaining may well

appear to be "over the top", it certainly does not seem so to the Georgians who host these banquets. For "In these celebrations of life and of their bonds to each other, they have discovered a uniquely effective way of making life bearable under the most adverse circumstances" (Tuite, 1995, p.13). We need to bear in mind that up until only recently life was nothing but grim for most of the people and this would have been one of the few ways available to them of escaping from it all.

At the start of the harvest each year people used to celebrate the event. One day everyone is out, dressed up and working in the fields, but doing nothing too arduous because it is a time for celebration. Among those people there are three poor brothers who have no food and only a little araq'i (chacha) to drink. Everyone is sitting down for dinner. They are feasting and singing.

Suddenly an old man came and said gamarjoba (hello) to everyone but nobody invited him to the table. When he passed by the three brothers, the youngest brother said:

"Let's invite him."

The brothers said:

"What can we offer him to eat or drink?"

"We can offer him what we have."

He did not ask again. Instead he called the man.

"Could you please honor us by coming to join us for a short time?"

The guest said:

"Everyone is feasting and singing. Why aren't you?"

"What can we do? We have no food, and only very little drink. How can we feast?"

The guest told the youngest brother:

"Not to worry. Pour whatever you do have and let's drink."

The youngest brother poured the drinks. And it's a wonderful wine!

"You don't have bread, do you?" asked the guest, and then, "Can you see something white on that mountain? What is that then? Go and bring it here!"

"That's a stone. Why should I bring it here?"

"Go and bring it and then you'll see why!"

The youngest brother went to the mountain. He saw a beautiful big sheep and white bread. Now the brothers can really lay the table. They sat down and started singing. They were singing so well that others stopped what they were doing to listen to them. Who are those singing this way!

The workers are laughing:

"What on earth could they have, that they have even been able to invite a quest! Those beggars are so poor that it's hard to imagine what they could give him to eat or drink."

When they had finished eating, and everyone was full, the old man asked the oldest brother:

"What would you prefer to have? What do you like most of all?"

"I would like land to grow food on!"

"You'll have land and food, as much as you could possibly ever want, for as long as you don't get tired of having guests and entertaining them," and then he blessed the land.

Then the old guest asked the middle brother:

"What would you prefer to have? What do you like most of all?"

"I'd like cattle," said the middle brother.

"Nobody will have as many cattle as you. You'll have as many as you could possibly ever want, for as long as you don't get tired of having guests and entertaining them."

And finally he asked the same question to the youngest brother:

"What would you like most of all?"

"I'd like to have a wife who would love guests and hosts, who would look after the family," said the youngest brother.

"Oh dear, I only know two women like that in this world, one is already married and the other is getting married today. I'll try to change things, though, so she marries you instead."

Two brothers settled down there in that place. One brother had land and bread, the second one had cattle, and he took the youngest brother with him.

A son of one king is marrying a daughter of another king. It is their wedding day. The old man took wind and rain with him. And he went to the place where the reception was being held and asked the people who were assembled there:

"We don't have anywhere to stay tonight. Can we stay with you?"

The king was told about it but he refused to allow it:

"If I let strangers attend the wedding celebrations, it might cause problems. I won't let anyone in tonight and after that I'll decide if I'll let you in or not."

The old man kicked the door open and went in regardless, taking the younger brother with him. The table is laid. The bride and bridegroom are sitting together. The old man and the boy are sitting opposite the newlyweds. The old man told the boy:

"Go get the bridegroom from his seat and you sit down there."

The boy did as he was told. The king was furious:

"That's why I didn't want to let you in."

The old man said:

"Don't talk nonsense! The bride belongs to him, not the bridegroom."

The king got more furious.

"Let's bet on whether he is the rightful husband or not."

"What bet can there be? We don't need to bet because that woman is already married," said the king. But then he changed his mind and asked, "What kind of bet were you thinking of?"

"Let's give each of these men a branch of a vine, and see in whose hands the branch grows leaves, blossoms, and then produces grapes which ripen and that we would then be able to eat at the table. And we'll give the wife to that person."

The king was reluctant to agree, but there was no way of going back by then and he knew it. So he gave both men a branch of a vine. In the hands of the younger brother the branch sprouted leaves, blossomed, produced grapes, and the grapes ripened. But the branch of the king's son remained as dry as a bone.

"Will you give the girl to the younger brother now?" asked the old man.

"No, I won't. She's already married."

"Then let's give it to the man who can dance on this sword."

The king's son was the first to get up and dance, but each time he stepped on the blade of the sword he cut his feet.

"Now it is your turn, to get up and dance," the old man told the younger brother.

The boy got up and danced on the sword without any problem.

"Now we can take the woman," the old man said to the king.

"No, you're not taking her, and that's final."

But the guests got up and left, and the woman got up too and left with them. Nobody could stop her. The old man helped them to settle down, blessed them and said:

"Nobody can ever be happier than the two of you unless there comes a point when you hate having guests."

Time passed and all the brothers lived happily. One day the same old man was passing by - he was St. George. It is raining; it is horrible out, such bad weather that nobody would wish to be out in it. The old man stands in front of the oldest brother.

"Show some charity! Let me stay with you. It's raining heavily outside."

"My wife burnt her hand by baking the bread for the last guests we had and, because of that, this time I won't let anyone in," said the oldest brother.

"Whatever fortune you had before, you will have the same

again," said the old man.

Then he stands in front of the middle brother's door and says:

"Show some charity! Let me stay with you. It's raining heavily outside."

My wife burnt her hand by baking the bread for the last guests we had and, because of that, this time I won't let anyone in," the middle brother answered the same way the oldest had.

"Whatever fortune you had before, you will have the same again," said the old man.

At last the old man stands in front of the younger brother's door. Only his wife is at home. Her husband has just died and she is at the side of his coffin crying.

"Hostess, hostess, good woman, let me stay with you tonight."

The saddened woman looked out:

"Do come in, please, and I will sweep the floor in a minute."

The woman wiped the tears from her eyes, hid the coffin in a dark corner, tidied up the house, started the fire, killed a hen and invited the guest in.

"Oh, I didn't know that you were alone. Where's your husband?" the old man asked.

"Yes, I am on my own at the moment. My husband went to the market, and he hasn't come back yet," said the sad woman.

The guest knows that her husband is dead and that he is in the coffin in the dark corner of the room. The guest got up pretending that he wanted to go out. He went to the dark corner, lifted up the lid of the coffin, blew his breath over him, and the youngest brother came back to life again. And this time he was even better looking than he had been before. The old man held him by the hand and they went into the room

"Why were you so late?" asked the woman, trying not to show the guest her true feelings.

"I already know everything. You're a very good woman and you will have a great fortune," said the old man. He blessed the youngest brother and his wife, said goodbye, and left.

Ever since that time, the youngest brother has become richer and happier, but his brothers poorer and poorer, and also more unhappy.

(Taken from Virsaladze, E. (1984) *Folktales of the World: Georgian Folktales*, Tbilisi: Nakaduli Publishing).

In ancient Georgian cosmology, the universe is sphere-shaped and consists of three vertically superposed worlds or *skneli*: the highest world or *zeskneli* is above the earth and is populated by the gods; the lowest world or *qveskneli* is below the earth and is the netherworld populated by demons, evil spirits and dragons; in between these two worlds in the earthly world with humans, animals, plants, etc. Each of these three worlds has its own color, white for the highest, red for the middle and black for the lowest. Beyond this universe is *gareskneli* or the world of oblivion, darkness and eternity. There are two bodies of water and fire, celestial and subterranean, which have unique properties and affect human lives differently. The sun makes its voyage between the two extreme worlds, the celestial and the subterranean. The moon makes the same journey as the sun but in the opposite direction and rhythm. The moon and the sun are, respectively, brother and sister. The earthly world has a center which divides it into two regions, anterior (*tsina samkaro, tsinaskneli*) and posterior (*ukana samkaro or ukanaskneli*). The three vertical worlds are separated by ether but they are connected by the Tree of Life that grows on the edge of the universe; (in some versions, a tower, chain or pillar). The various lands of the earthly world are usually separated by seven or nine mountains or seas. To travel between these lands a hero must undergo a spiritual transformation (*gardacvaleba*) and seek help of magical animals, i.e. Rashi, Paskunji, etc. After the spread of Christianity, pagan cosmology amalgamated the Christian teachings. The *zeskneli* became heaven and abode of the Trinity while *qveskneli* turned into hell and abode of devil. The spiritual travel to these worlds became associated with death (taken from Georgia: Past, Present, Future *http://rustaveli.tripod.com/mythology.html* [accessed 23/11/08]).

Although the traditional Georgian religion is commonly described as polytheistic, in fact this is a fallacy as there is a clear distinction between the Supreme God (*Morige Ghmerti*), creator and sustainer of the universe, and all other divine beings, as there is in other so-called polytheistic religions such as Yoruba. And many of the deities have taken on Christian names, as is the case with Santeria in Brazil for example, so that as in some parts of Europe what we find is that the worship of particular saints was actually founded upon the worship of pagan deities.

Among the principal figures are "St. George" (*Giorgi*; in Svan *Jgëræg*), the "Archangel" (Georgian *Mtavarangelozi*; Svan *Taringzel*), and a hunter deity and protector of wildlife in the high mountains (in Svaneti represented as the goddess *Dæl* or *Dali*). Important female figures include *Barbal* "St. Barbara," a fertility deity and healer of illnesses; and *Lamaria* "St. Mary," protector of women. *Krist'e* "Christ" presides over the world of the dead (Tuite, 1995, p.14).

An Old Guest, which can perhaps best be described as a moralistic tale, features St. George, who is considered to be the Georgian nation's protector. It is said that Giorgi was a member of the personal guard attached to Roman Emperor Diocletian. In

303, Diocletian issued an edict authorizing the systematic persecution of Christians across the Empire and Giorgi was ordered to
take part in the process. Instead, however, he confessed to being
a Christian himself and criticized the imperial decision. This
enraged Diocletian who then ordered the torture of the "traitor"
on a wheel, and this was followed by his execution. The Georgian
Orthodox Church marks St. Giorgi's Day on November 23 each
year, the day of his torture.

Of particular interest in connection with *An Old Guest* is that
in the Georgian New Year ritual, the ritual guest who steps over
the threshold of the house and represents the messenger of the
God becomes visible as the personified character of St. Basil, St.
George, or the Lord. It would thus appear to be the case that the
St. George in our tale, who asks to be invited into the houses of
the three brothers, could well be the very same character.

In her paper 'The Spatial-temporal Patterns of Georgian
Winter Solstice Festivals' Nino Abakelia describes how, as
defined by van Gennep and later by the anthropologist Victor
Turner, the New Year can be regarded as a liminal phenomenon
from the perspective of both space and time. "This is a period of
the year when the thresholds of the inner and outer worlds
become vulnerable and, as a result, open for the various
undesirable and desirable powers and forces which can penetrate
through these passages" (Abakelia, 2008, p.104). To prevent
accidents from happening or for protection against them, certain
rituals would be performed. These included, on New Year's Day,
inviting a ritual guest to step over the threshold of the house.

The first ritual guest who was to step over the threshold of the
house on New Year's Day was called mek'vle (the one who leaves
traces or footprints), and had been tested beforehand on St.
Barbara's Day (Dec 4/17). "On that day, a person was invited to
visit the house and bless the household. The special guests were
invited with the aim to avoid a random "unlucky foot" stepping
into the house. If the guest's "foot" was approved, he would be

invited to return on the New Year's Day as a first-foot" (Abakelia, 2008, p. 108).

For Georgians, the start of the first day (week, month, or the New Year) is considered to be of particular importance as a good beginning is believed to set the right tone for what follows. The responsibility for ensuring this took place fell upon the first-foot, and the role he plays, that of a benevolent angel, is expressed in the New Year's congratulation formula that he recites:

I enter the house,
Let everybody be blessed by the Lord,
Let my footprints be like those of the angels
(With my angel's foot,
I share the blessings of the Lord) (Abakelia, 2008, p. 108).

A distinction is made between the "inner" first-foot, who is elected among the members of the family, and the "outer" first-foot, who is the person specially chosen and invited to the house in order to ensure a favorable year. The belief is that if this is not done, an unexpected guest might arrive who would not be safe for the family.

Preparations for the ritual were started by the chosen first-foot on New Year's Eve when he would look for a branch of a hazelnut tree, a Georgian symbol of fecundity. From this he would craft what was known as a chichilak'i, which represented the tree of life and the axis of the world. The hazelnut tree stick was warmed over a fire and peeled so that the shavings were left hanging on it.

Two horizontal crosses were attached to the stick: one on the foot and the other on the top of it. A wicker wreath decorated with leaves of ivy, plants with small red and black berries, mistletoe branches and other evergreen plants were attached to the top of the tree and a loaf of ritual bread called boqeli ...

was put over it. At the two ends of the horizontal cross, balls of dough about the size of apples were fixed. The balls were called qvinchila ('cockerels'). On the remaining two ends, an apple and a pomegranate were attached. Next to these 'cockerels' a plucked songbird (the messenger of Lord) was hung. Feathers were left on its tail and wings, and sometimes only the tail was hung as the sign of the songbird ... All these were manifestations of the upper world as well as fecundity symbols. Sometimes the tree was decorated with silver coins, colorful bands, candies and jewels. ... The cockerels and the bird symbolized the celestial world and kind spiritual beings. Sometimes, this sacred tree was also called Basil's/Vasil's beard (Abakelia, 2008, p. 109).

There is also an association with the sun, with the ritual bread on the top of the chichilak'i representing the sun itself and the wood shaving hanging from it representing the rays, as well as lightning (celestial fire) and rain, which fertilize the earth. This would not be unusual as in many traditions the image of the sun is associated with the tree, with it being considered the "fruit" of the tree.

Early in the morning the first-foot, carrying various fecundity symbols and known as Basila, would call on the lady of the house and hold a dialogue with her:

-Open the door, fortunate one! (Would you, please, open the door!)
-What are you carrying (bringing) us, fortunate one?
-Good omens for everybody. The great God's mercy, kindness, the growth of cattle, filling of barns, stocks, and pigsty; jugs filled with wine in the wine-cellar, chest filled with silver coins and all the kindness, fortune, wellbeing, and peace. Open the door, fortunate one!

Only after the first-foot had repeated the blessing thrice,

the door would be opened. The first-foot who stepped into the house with his right foot first (the symbol guaranteeing success in any kind of activity) blessed the house and members of the household with the above formula and once again assured the residents that he was the one (of the holy beings) to bring ill or good omens with the following words, "I am entering the house. Let my footprints be the traces of the Angel!" This holy being was usually represented by Basila (Abakelia, 2008, p. 111).

The name Basila is generally agreed to refer to St. Basil the Great, Bishop of Caesarea, whose feast day falls on January 1st. However, it is also possible the first-foot could have been named Basila after a pagan fertility deity known under various names including Beri, Bombgha, Bambghu, Boseli, and Boslam.

There were also other visitors, called berik'as, who were represented by a group of young mummers, mostly boys, who wore sheepskins inside out and whose faces were smeared with soot. The group would each family in the village and be treated with bread, eggs, sweets, money, etc. In return, as long as they were treated generously, they would bless each family. If not, the family would be cursed. While this was taking place, members of the households they visited would attempt to pluck out some wool from the berik'as' sheepskins and hide it somewhere as it was supposed to bring fecundity or the coming year. At one time the ritual called berik'aoba had been performed during a spring festival dedicated to the cult of a dying and resurrecting vegetative deity, but once the Julian calendar was introduced, it was doubled in January to celebrate the New Year too.

Another ritual, called lipanali or sulebis gadabrdzaneba 'sending off the spirits' ... occurred annually on the Epiphany and lasted for about a week. During this period, tables were covered for the berikas in houses or in special farm constructions and the ancestral chair of the head of the kin was placed at the table; the oldest man who was the head of the family was to serve them with his head uncovered (as an expression of respect).

Of all the rituals this was the most mysterious. It was performed in absolute silence. Nobody was allowed to be present during the secret prayer in which only the spirits of the dead ancestors and the head of the family participated. The rest of the family was allowed to join the meal only after the ritual prayer was over. After the "prescribed time", the guests had to leave their living relatives by performing a ritual. The head of the family prepared for this day a glass of wine, a piece of cooked meat and a slice of bread. Holding all these in his hands, partially bent, he "accompanied" the invisible guests and saw them off through the gate repeating all the way the words: "This way, please!" During the walk he poured wine libation on the ground and by the time he reached the gate the glass would be empty. Then he opened the gate and placed the bread and meat on a stone nearby. Then he would haste home without looking back (reciting traditional taboos with regard to the deceased). ... Thus the spirits of the dead were sent off, the necessary order was established and the society was ready to restart its everyday life (Abakelia, 2008, p. 113).

Bibliography

Abakelia, N. (2008) 'The Spatial-temporal Patterns of Georgian Winter Solstice Festivals' In *Folklore* 40. Pp. 101- 116

Dolidze N.I. (1999) *Georgian Folk Tales*, Tbilisi: Merani Publishing House.

Tuite, K. (ed.) (1995) *Violet on the Mountain: An Anthology of Georgian Folk Poetry*, Tbilisi: Amirani.

Dzyzlan, the Mother of Water
& the Origins of Tbilisi

There are many stories in mythology and folklore about marriage or union between mortals and water-spirits, and the one presented here comes from Abkhazia. It was taken from Bgazhba, Kh.S. (1985) *Abkhazian Tales*, Translated from the Russian, with new Introduction by D.G. Hunt. (Russian edition published by Alashara Publishing House, Sukhumi).

Dzyzlan

Have you heard of Dzyzlan, the Mother of Water? If you have not heard of her, this is what they tell of her. She is a water maiden, a beauty with long golden hair. Her feet are turned backwards, and for that reason, in wrestling with her, nobody can manage to throw her down on her back. She swims well; in water she feels as if she is at home. Her body is elastic; her skin is white, like amsyr-kyaadysh [papyrus]. And her eyes sparkle, like diamonds.

The mother of Dzyzlan, Akhidzakhuazhv the Golden, the Mistress of the Waters, educated her daughter in her own image; she gave her her own beauty and habits. Dzyzlan has the habit of pestering lone travelers, men, and she enters into a wrestling bout with them. Sometimes she falls in love with young and handsome people. She is not afraid of any sort of weapon, except for a double-edged *kinzhal* [a Caucasian long-bladed knife]. On meeting her, a traveler must unsheathe his *kinzhal* and, raising it, pronounce, "Uashkhua makyapsys" [a magic expression, literally: Uashkhua (a deity), makyapsys – a soft whetstone]. Then she submits. But most of all she prizes her golden hair.

Dzyzlan goes into the service of the one who manages to pull out or cut off a lock of her hair. A pistol and a gun are useless against her; they misfire. Nor does a sword frighten her, she catches it by the handle. So this is what Dzyzlan is like!

One day, a hero was riding through the forest to be entertained by his relatives. It was already evening and drizzling; the very time for Dzyzlan's tricks. He rode up to the river and began to look for a ford. Suddenly his horse began to snort and stopped. However much he urged it on, however much he drove it, it would not move from the spot. The rider looks, and in front of him stands the beauty, Dzyzlan. The rider asks her, "What do you want?", but she does not answer.

Dzyzlan threw herself on him. She pulled him off his horse, and entered into a wrestling bout with him. For a long time they fought. Dzyzlan began to get tired. She dragged him to the stream, but the hero was ready for her: he pulled out his *kinzhal* and cut off a lock of the beauty's hair, and he hid it in his little pocket for *gazyre* [a small cylindrical wooden case for powder or cartridges]. Dzyzlan became submissive and went to him. The hero picked her up and set her in front of him on his saddle bow. And thus he brought her home.

Dzyzlan went into service for him and did everything about the house. Every day she asked him to return her hair, but the master did not give it to her. He hid Dzyzlan's hair under a rafter of the roof. One day, everyone had gone off to the field to work. At home there remained only Dzyzlan and a little girl. Dzyzlan boiled up a big pot of milk, treated the girl to the cream, and then began to pump her: where is her, Dzyzlan's, hair? The little girl pointed under the rafter. Dzyzlan got the lock of her hair. She started laughing, then she seized the little girl and threw her into the pot with the boiling milk, while she herself escaped.

They tell also about another incident. The famous hunter Akun-Ipa Khatazhukva met Dzyzlan in the valley of the River Aaldzga. He beat her in wrestling, he cut off a lock of her hair, he sewed it up into some leather and then wore it like an amulet on his chest. She began asking him to let her go. Akun-Ipa demanded from her a promise that from then on she would not trouble people, neither in the day nor in the night. Dzyzlan gave her promise: "May your bullet never miss its target and may I be impotent to cause mischief to men-travelers that I meet". Akun-Ipa gave Dzyzlan her hair and let her go.

From then on the hunter never had a miss. His bullet overtook any game which he was not too lazy to shoot at. So that is the way in which Akun-Ipa Khatazhukva became a great hunter.

From that time Dzyzlan became harmless to solitary men-travelers. If it happened that she caught sight of a man, she made a large detour round him. That is why Dzyzlan ceased to be seen or heard.

They say that, in olden times, young women getting married

would make prayers, to establish good relations with the Mother of Water.

Evidence of the importance of hunting in the history and culture of the Georgian races is present in numerous historical records, ancient books, ethnographical material, and specialized research. ... According to old beliefs, sylvan and mountain animals had a patron or protector of their own, upon whom the hunter's "success" mainly depended. This patron might exist in the form of a tiger, deer, bird or snake (Virsaladze, 1976, p.357).

It would seem to be the case that for Akun-Ipa Khatazhukva, it was Dzyzlan who fulfilled this role. A large number of myths and legends feature a semi-divine woman in the form of a nymph or a fairy who acts as a teacher, helping the hero through the difficulties of what are often initiatory ordeals and by showing him how to gain possession of the symbol of immortality or long life (see Eliade, 1964, p.78). In this particular case, the semi-divine figure shows the hero how to have success in hunting.

The Waters have been described as the reservoir of all the potentialities of existence because they not only precede every form but they also serve to sustain every creation. Immersion is equivalent to dissolution of form, in other words death, whereas emergence repeats the cosmogonic act of formal manifestation, in other words rebirth (see Eliade, 1952, p.151).

In whatever religious context we find it, water invariably serves the function of dissolving the forms of things, and it can be seen to be both purifying and regenerative. "The purpose of the ritual lustrations and purifications is to gain a flash of realization of the non-temporal moment ... in which the creation took place; they are symbolical repetitions of the birth of worlds or of the "new man" " (Eliade, 1952, p.152).

One of the attributes often credited to shamans, as well as to witches and other kinds of magical practitioner, is the ability to shape-shift from human into animal shape. Sometimes this change is a literal one, human flesh transformed into animal flesh or covered over by animal skin; in other accounts, the soul leaves the shaman's unconscious body to enter into the body of an animal, fish or bird. And it is not only shamans who have such powers according to tales from around the globe. Shape shifting is part of a mythic and storytelling tradition stretching back over thousands of years. The gods of various mythologies are credited with this ability, as are the heroes of the great epic sagas.

In Nordic myth, Odin could change his shape into any beast or bird; in Greek myth, Zeus often assumed animal shape in his relentless pursuit of young women. Cernunnos, the lord of animals in Celtic mythology, wore the shape of a stag, and also the shape of a man with a heavy rack of horns. In the *Odyssey*, Homer tells the tale of Proteus - a famous soothsayer who would not give away his knowledge unless forced to do so. Menelaus came upon him while he slept, and held on to him tightly as he shape-shifted into a lion, a snake, a leopard, a bear, etc. Defeated, Proteus returned to his own shape and Menelaus won the answers to his questions.

Not all transformations are from human to animal shape. *The Great Selkie of Sule Skerry,* described in Scottish ballads, is a man upon dry land, a *selkie* [seal] in the sea, and he leaves a human maid pregnant with his child. And Irish legends tell of men who marry seal or otter women and then hide their animal skins from them to prevent them from returning to the water. Generally these women bear several sons, but pine away for their true home. If they manage to find the skin, they then return to the sea with barely a thought for the ones left behind. As for Dzyzlan, it would seem from all accounts that she has the power to appear to man as a seductive temptress.

In Tibet, a frog-husband is an unexpected source of joy to a shy young bride. He is not a man disguised as a frog but a frog disguised as a man. When his young wife burns his frog skin to keep her lover in the shape she prefers, the frog-husband loses his magical powers, gracefully resigning himself to ordinary human life instead.

The Japanese story *The Robe of Feathers* is about a tennyo - a nymph clad in fluttering veils and without wings who roams in the sky. Such beings are also said to surround pious Buddhists for whom they perform the duties of ministering angels. The tennyo's robe is known as a hagoromo. In Watase's version of the tale, *Ayashi no Ceres*, the hagoromo is not needed to fly or to give the tennyo magical abilities (she possesses those abilities in any case). Instead the robe, by making her beautiful, helps the tennyo attract husbands and to produce descendants. It is also said that the hagoromo is their manna, and if the robe is not returned to them, the tennyo die.

In *The Robe of Feathers* the meeting between the fisherman who is attracted by the tennyo and the spirit is short-lived but in other tales it leads to marriage. The Japanese tales of marriages between humans and spirits are varied, ranging from the marriage of Yuki-onna The Snow Woman (a female mountain spirit) to a mortal, to those in which mortals couple with spirits of the vegetable world - as in the story of the spirit of the Willow Tree (see Piggot, 1982, p.71). The well-known tale of *Urashima* (see Berman, 2007) provides another example of the genre. There are also Japanese fairy tales that warn of the danger of *kitsune*, the fox-wife. The fox takes on the form of a beautiful woman in these stories, but to wed her brings madness and death.

While on the subject of the significance of water in Georgian folklore, it is worth mentioning that the name of the capital *Tbilisi* derives from the Old Georgian word "Tpili", meaning warm, which is a reference to the waters located there. According to an old legend, as late as 458 AD, the present-day territory of Tbilisi was covered by forests. King Vakhtang I Gorgasali is said to have gone hunting in the heavily wooded region with a falcon, which caught and injured a pheasant. The falcon then dropped the injured pheasant and it fell into a hot spring. As a result of its immersion in the water, it miraculously recovered and it flew away as good as new. King Vakhtang became so impressed with the hot springs that he decided to cut down the forest and build a city on the location, and the name *Tbilisi* ("warm location") was given to it because of the area's numerous sulfuric hot springs.

Interestingly, as Constantine Lerner (2001) points out, the main element of the plot in the legend resembles the legendary motif of the "river of paradise" which in ancient Jewish folkloristic tradition was associated with Alexander the Great.

A version of the legend can be found in the Jewish cycle of the romance – in *An Old Hebrew Romance of Alexander Mucdon*. This work is extant in three manuscripts from the 10th-12th centuries: from Damascus (Harkavi 1892), Modena (Levi 1896) and Oxford (Gaster 1897), though the romance itself was created much earlier, already in the pre-Islamic period (Gaster 1897: 411).... : *On his return* [from Afriqi and Qartinia] *Alexander sat by a certain spring eating bread. One of the king's hunters caught some birds, and after killing them, washed them in the water of this river, but when he put them in the water in order to wash them, they came to life and flew away [—-] The king exclaimed that it must be the water of the Garden of Eden [—-]* (Gaster, 1897, p.531; cited in Lerner, 2001, p.73).

The parallelism becomes even clearer when we consider another version of the Georgian legend about the origins of Tbilisi, in which a deer instead of a pheasant is the object of the hunt:

King Vakhtang Gorgasal was hunting in the forest. He shot an arrow at a deer. The deer jumped into a hot spring and made a sound and became well again and ran away (Lerner, 2001, p.74).

In view of the similarities, Lerner argues it could well be the case that "there existed an ancient Semitic layer in the cultural history of Georgia" (Lerner, 2001, p.77). Whether this ancient Semitic layer exists or not is debatable. However, what is clear from all the material presented above is that the waters can be said to "symbolize the entire universe of the virtual; they are the *fons et origo*, the reservoir of all the potentialities of existence; they precede every form and sustain every creation" (Eliade, 1991, p.151). And this applies in Georgian folklore and mythology just as much as it does in the folklore and mythology of other cultures.

Bibliography

Ascherson, N. (2007) *Black Sea: The Birthplace of Civilisation and Barbarism*, London: Vintage Books.

Berman, M. (2007) *Soul Loss and the Shamanic Story*, Newcastle: Cambridge Scholars Publishing.

Bgazhba, Kh.S. (1985) *Abkhazian Tales*, Translated from the Russian, with new Introduction by D.G. Hunt. (Russian edition published by Alashara Publishing House, Sukhumi).

Eliade, M. (1991) *Images and Symbols*, New Jersey: Princeton University Press (The original edition is copyright Librairie Gallimard 1952).

Hewitt, G. (ed.) (1999) *The Abkhasians*: A Handbook, Richmond, Surrey: Curzon Press

Gaster, M. (1897) 'An Old Hebrew Romance of Alexander'. In *Journal of theRoyal Asiatic Society*, July. London, pp. 485–549.

Lerner, C.B. (2001) 'The "River of Paradaise" and the legend about the city of Tbilisi: A Literary Source of the Legend'. In *Folklore Vol. 16*, published by the Folk Belief and Media Group of ELM. Electronic version ISSN 1406-0949 is available from *http://haldjas.folklore.ee/folklore*

Piggot, J. (1982) *Japanese Mythology*, London: Hamlyn.

The Tale of a King's Son

There was one king who had three children, all sons. When he got older he started to lose his eyesight.

"Which of my sons deserves to become a king? I need to decide," he said, and ordered his oldest son to come to him. The king asked him:

"What is the fattest, fastest and the most beautiful? I want to test you to find out if you're the right person to become the next king, and if I should leave my kingdom to you."

The king, I should mention, had a beautiful horse.

"Your horse is the fattest of all, your wife (my mother) is the most beautiful, and your hound is the fastest."

"No, my son. You don't deserve my kingdom I'm afraid. Go," he said.

He ordered his middle son to come and asked him the same question.

"My wife is the most beautiful, my horse is the fattest and my hound is the fastest."

"No, my son, you too don't deserve to be the next king."

Then he ordered his youngest son to come.

"Nothing is more beautiful than spring, more fruitful than autumn or faster than the eyes with which we are born. An eye can see everything around it in less than the time it takes to blink."

The father held his hand with joy and said:

"You're the one who deserves to be king and you're the one who's going to bring me the cure for my affliction – the special medicine that will restore my eyesight."

The son said:

"I'll think about it, and if I can do it I will"

Now the king had a wise horse, and the wise horse spoke to the youngest son:

"Ask your father to make a special saddle for me from the skin of a deer, a saddle with nine decorations, and to give you a good sword. Ask him too for such a whip, that when you hit me three layers of my skin will come off. Then I will run so fast that nobody can see me – and I will fly up into the sky. When I come down to earth again, you need to start digging exactly at that spot. You will find the cure for your father's problem there. But you need to be quick to catch it; otherwise it will be lost to you."

The boy did as he was told, and when the horse landed again on the earth, he started to dig the ground there. Suddenly what looked like a leather pouch shot out from the hole he had dug, which must have contained his father's medicine, but it came out so fast that it was impossible for the boy to catch it and it flew up into the sky.

"The pouch containing the medicine will fall down from the sky in exactly a year's time on the same day as today," the horse said. "Meanwhile, the king of the east is fighting with the king of the west. The king of the west is losing but we can help him by fighting in his army."

The boy looks and sees that the army of the king of the east is approaching. The dark dust raised by the marching soldiers follows the army like a shadow. The boy and the horse started fighting. Between them, they killed many of the soldiers, and the king and his personal servants ran away defeated. The horse killed them with his hooves and the boy with his sword. Meanwhile, the king of the west, who had been expecting the enemy, looks out on to the battlefield from the ramparts of his castle. He sees everything that happens and says:

"Who is this man, intent on helping me, who has defeated my enemy?"

The boy cut his little finger in the fight and asked the King:

"Can you give me some kind of dressing to bandage my little finger with?"

He was not only given a dressing to bandage his finger with, but he was given his own private room to rest in too. As for his horse, he was given his own special stable, his back was covered with warm woolen blankets, and he was fed not on hay (as horses normally are) but on the very best almonds and raisins. The king's servants saw all this and became very jealous - he can become close to the king because he is such a good person - was what they thought. So they went to the king and told him:

"That boy's so special that he can even build you a castle from elephants' bones."

The king told the boy this at breakfast and asked him if it was true. The boy, after thinking for a while, said:

"I'll tell you the answer tomorrow." Then he went and asked his horse.

"That's easy," said the horse. "Ask the king to give you one hundred sap'alne (a measurement of weight, equal to 480 kg) of wool, one hundred sap'alne (500 liters) of wine, and we can build him a castle from elephants' bones without any problem."

The youngest brother told the king. He was given what he had asked for and then he set out for the country where the elephants lived. When the boy and the horse reached that country, they saw a beautiful mountain. Nine streams were coming out from nine different sources, and all the elephants were drinking the water. The boy used the wool to block up all the outlets so the water took a different route. With the rest of the wool and the stones they made a pond, which they filled with the wine they had brought with them for the purpose. Then they withdrew and waited.

"Have a look to see if the elephants are gathering together or if they're lying down," said the horse.

"They're gathering together," said the boy.

"So they are coming then."

The boy and the horse hid themselves. The elephants arrive, drink from the pond filled with wine, get drunk, and all fall down.

"Now use your sword and cut their throats." The horse himself did the same. They killed all the elephants, and then cleaned the meat from the bones. With the help of two hundred horses, they took the bones of the elephants with them. The rest of the bones they left there, planning to return for them on another occasion. When they arrived home, the servants all had a shock because they had been hoping that the boy would be killed. The boy and the horse started to build a beautiful castle using golden nails. The king is very pleased with what he sees. That night the servants went to him again.

"What a great person you found! And he can bring you the king of the birds to this beautiful castle too. We can hang the cage with the bird in the castle and the whole world will be amazed.

The king ordered the youngest bother to come to him and said:

"Bring me the king of the birds next!"

"I'll think about that and let you know the answer tomorrow." The boy went to the horse that night.

"He told me to bring him the king of the birds this time."

"Not to worry about that. Ask him to give you nine sap'alne of grain and we will bring him the bird then, just as he asks."

They were given the grain and the boy and the horse set out together again. They eventually reached a strange mountain, where you could hear the singing of any bird you wanted to.

"Now you lie down and scatter the grain all over your body. When the birds come to you, the king of the birds will sit exactly over your heart."

As soon as the boy lies down, the king of the birds comes and a great number of other birds follow him singing. The king of the birds pecks at the grain once, twice, and the third time the boy catches him. The boy was instructed to do so by the horse. When he caught the king of the birds, all the other birds started to beat him with their wings and scratch his face with their claws, but the horse came and frightened them off. Then he took the boy and returned to the castle with him.

The servants were surprised once again;

"How did he manage to come back this time?"

Once more they went to the king and said:

"Let him bring you a wife - Dunia from Nigozeti (the Land where Walnut Trees grow). If he is a hero, that should be no problem for him either."

The King called the youngest son and told him:

"Next you have to bring me Dunia from Nigozeti."

The boy went and asked the horse once again what to do.

"This time it will be very difficult," said the horse, "and I'm not sure if I can do that. The reason for saying this is: that woman has a horse, my sister, and she is better and faster than me. She might defeat me. Let's go anyway. We don't need to take anything with us, but I'm very frightened. That woman is sitting in a castle. The east door of that castle is open, but the west door is closed. She has a goat tied up with a bone in front of it, and she has a wolf tied up with hay in front of it. My sister, the horse, is also tied up there. You need to be quick to close the east door behind you once you enter, then to open the west door, throw the hay to the goat, and the bone to the wolf. I will try to hold my sister while you do that. The woman is there too. She has very long hair, and you need to reach for her hair quickly and tightly wind it round your hand."

The boy did as he was told by the horse. He wound her hair tightly round his hand and pulled her. The woman shouted:

"Door of the east, help me!"

"At last my hinges are closed and I'm having a rest," said the eastern door. She called to the western door then:

"Door of the west, help me!"

"At last my hinges are open and I'm breathing fresh air once again."

Then she called to the horse:

"Help me!"

"I'm competing with my sister and I have no time for you."

The boy made the woman obey him, sat her on the horse, and they left. The woman then said:

"I cannot see the king yet. Build a marble bath for me - I have to have a milk bath."

The milk was brought and boiled.

"I want the king to come out now."

The king came out and the woman said to him:

"Please, you have to have a bath first!"

When the king went to the edge of the bath, she pushed him into the boiling milk and the king died. Then they threw all the servants into the bath too. The boy was left with the east and west kingdoms and also with the wife, Dunia from Nigozeti. Then the time arrived when the leather pouch with the medicine for his father's eyes was due to fall down from the sky. With the help of the horse, the boy managed to catch it, just in time, before it hit the ground. The boy took the woman and returned to his father the king with her, who was delighted to see his son again.

Father, I've bought you the medicine for your eyes, I became the king of two other kingdoms in the process, and I've also found myself a wife.

The son was very happy and his father arranged a big wedding reception for him.

(Taken from Virsaladze, E. (1984) *Folktales of the World: Georgian Folktales*, Tbilisi: Nakaduli Publishing).

As in so many stories from the Caucasus, and as in folktales from other cultures too, once again we see the importance attached to the number three – three brothers and the three quests the youngest brother is set. Again and again in stories "we see how things appear in threes: how things have to happen three times, how the hero is given three wishes; how Cinderella goes to the ball three times; how the hero or the heroine is the third of three children" (Booker, 2004, p.229). Pythagoras called three the perfect number in that it represented the beginning, the middle and the end, and he thus regarded it as a symbol of Deity.

As for the mountain with nine streams, three times three represents a trinity of trinities. The Pythagoreans believed that man is a full chord, or eight notes, and deity comes next. Three is the perfect trinity and represents perfect unity, twice three is the perfect dual, and three times three is the perfect plural, which explains why nine was considered to be a mystical number. Our tale certainly has a mystical element to it, and its connection to such symbolism clearly gives it greater significance. However, to suggest that the comparison with a trinity of trinities was intentional on the part of its author is perhaps, though interesting, a bit too far-fetched. One of the problems when it comes to considering symbolism is symbolic meaning can be read into almost anything and there is often no way of checking the interpretation.

The number nine is significant for another reason too. The supreme divinity, head of the pantheon of gods, chief architect and lord of the universe is known as Ghmerti. All-powerful, it is said that he created the universe and that he lives on the ninth sky, where he resides on a golden throne. His daughter, the Sun, and son, the Moon, illuminate the earth while his other offspring, *khvtis-shvilni*, wander the earth, protecting humans and fighting the evil forces. Ghmerti controls nature and animals and he determines the length and events of every human's life. Ghmerti often was called *Morige Ghmerti* ("God the Director") or *Dambadebeli* ("the Creator"). Following the spread of Christianity, the cult of Ghmerti quickly merged with the identity of God the Father and the word "ghmerti" is still used in the Christian tradition.

The human-horse relationship is clearly an important one "in a region with extensive uninhabited areas, in which one's horse may have literally meant the difference between life and death" (Dolidze, 1999, p.9), and the connection felt between mountaineer and horse in Georgia is probably as ancient as their myths. There is, for example, a Georgian legend that asks, "Who were my ancestors?" And the answer given is "He who pulled milk out of a wild mare's udder with his lips and grew drunk as a little foal". Consequently, the fact that the horse plays such a significant role in this particular story would come as no surprise to anyone familiar with both the geography and history of the land.

> Pre-eminently the funerary animal and psychopomp, the "horse" is employed by the shaman, in various contexts, as a means of achieving ecstasy, that is, the "coming out of oneself" that makes the mystical journey possible. The "horse" enables the shaman to fly through the air, to reach the heavens. The dominant aspect of the mythology of the horse is not infernal but funerary; the horse is a mythical image of death and hence is incorporated into the ideologies and techniques of ecstasy. The horse carries the deceased into the beyond; it produces the "break-through in plane", the passage from this world to other worlds (Eliade, 1964, p.467).

However, the infernal direction, contrary to what Eliade suggests, is not necessarily to the Lower World, just as Heaven is not necessarily only found in the sky. Moreover, the horse in this particular folktale would seem to play a rather different role to the one Eliade describes, as it plays the role of a spirit helper and guide, showing the misunderstanding that can result from making such sweeping generalizations as we are presented with here.

We also know that times long since past, there was a custom of sacrificing horses and burying them along with the dead, a habit probably shared with the Scythians, and many horse burials have been unearthed, especially in western Georgia (see Anderson, 2003, p.95). And Eliade, writing about the Altaic horse sacrifice, points out how "several Turkic peoples [and it should be remembered that Georgia's neighbors are Turkic peoples] practice the same horse sacrifice to the celestial being without having recourse to a shaman. Besides the Turko-Tatars, the horse sacrifice was practiced by the majority of Indo-European peoples, and always offered to a god of the sky or the storm" (Eliade, 1964, p.198).

The horse in this particular tale is a rashi, a magical winged horse. Rashis can be of different kinds. Those of land were well disposed to humans and heroes and could see the future. Rashis of the seas were more hostile to humans but could take heroes to the depth of the sea while their milk was believed to cure many illnesses. Heavenly rashis were winged and fire-breathing animals, very difficult to subdue but loyal to their riders.

The story is set in the days when men and animals still lived like friends and could speak, one to the other, in the same language, as the youngest son and the horse are able to do, in other words in the days of shamans. Shape-shifting can be viewed as the imitation of the actions and voices of animals, though the shaman himself would certainly not describe what he does in such terms. During his apprenticeship, the future shaman has to learn the secret language required to communicate with the animal spirits and how to take possession of them, and this is often the "animal language" itself or a form of language derived from animal cries. It is regarded as equivalent to knowing the secrets of nature and hence evidence of the ability to be able to prophesy. And by sharing in the animal mode of being, the shaman can be seen to be re-establishing the situation that existed in mythical times, when man and animal were one (see Eliade, 1989, pp.96-98).

As for Dunia from Nigozeti (the Land where the Walnut Trees Grow), the particularly attractive and impressive-looking Walnut Tree, which provides shade in the heat of the summer months, is indigenous to Georgia, and the nut itself is an important ingredient in Georgian cuisine. It is ground into a paste and used to make satsivi, for example, a sauce to prepare chicken in. It is also used to make nigvziani badrijani - fried eggplant slices covered with walnut paste, which are then garnished with pomegranate seeds.

Having problems getting into a castle which contains a beautiful woman, in this case the woman who is destined to become the youngest son's wife, is a fairly common motif in fairy stories (e.g. *Sleeping Beauty*) and it can be understood in terms of sexual imagery and loss of virginity too. Severance can be said to take place when the youngest son first sets off on his journey to find the cure for his father, entering the castle represents entering Sacred Space, and the return home from the journey represents the reincorporation stage of the three-stage ritual cycle. The cycle was first proposed by van Gennep and then later developed by the anthropologist Victor Turner in his work. Not only is this the form that most ceremonies can be seen to take, it is also the structure most shamanic stories are based on, just as this one is.

Eliade believed "myths and fairy tales were derived from, or give symbolic expression to, initiation rites or other *rites de passage*–such as a metaphoric death of an old, inadequate self in order to be reborn on a higher plane of existence" (Bettelheim, 1991, p.35). *The Tale of a King's Son* can be regarded as the account of the initiation rite of the king's youngest son. As for his wedding, "The permanent union of, for example, a prince and a princess symbolizes the integration of the disparate aspects of the personality – psychoanalytically speaking, the id, ego, and superego" (Bettelheim, 1991, p.146). Not only does such union symbolize moral unity on the highest plane but at the same time it can be seen as a means of restoring the balance of the community. In his or her role as an intermediary, "the shaman can be seen to be responsible for maintaining the balance of the community and for creating the harmony from which life springs" (Halifax, 1991, p.15). And, by the end of the tale, this is exactly what the youngest son has succeeded in ensuring.

Bibliography

Anderson, T. (2003) *Bread and Ashes: A Walk Through the Mountains of Georgia*, London: Jonathan Cape.

Bettelheim, B. (1991) *The Uses of Enchantment*, London: Penguin Books.

Booker, C. (2004) *The Seven Basic Plots: Why we tell Stories*, London: Continuum.

Dolidze, N.I. (1999) *Georgian Folk Tales*, Tbilisi: Merani Publishing House.

Eliade, M. (1964) *Myth and Reality*, London: George Allen & Unwin

Eliade, M.. (1989) *Shamanism: Archaic techniques of ecstasy*, London: Arkana (first published in the USA by Pantheon Books 1964).

Halifax, J. (1991) *Shamanic Voices*, London: Arkana (first published in 1979).

The Hunter's Son

There was and there was not, what can be better than God. There was a well-known hunter who was normally very successful at his job. One day, however, the hunter was in an empty field when suddenly a white deer appeared in front of him. The deer stood there face to face with him and this is what he said:

"Shoot me! If you hit me – lucky you and if you miss – poor you!"

The hunter shoots but misses, and the deer disappears. The hunter went home and told his wife:

"Today I shot at a white deer and missed. This means I'm about to die so prepare my shroud and order my coffin please."

The hunter died the very same night. His wife got pregnant and gave a birth to a boy. The boy was so strong and quick that there was nobody else like him in the world. One day the son took his father's gun down from where it hung, loaded it with bullets, went to his mother's room and asked her:

"What did my father die for?"

"Fate," replied the mother.

"No, you have to tell me the truth," insisted the son. In the end the mother told him everything.

The son got up, made a target on a tree, fired three times and all the bullets hit it, right in the centre. Then, with the gun slung over his shoulder, he set off to search for the deer.

He passed through the forest on his way, past all the trees, until eventually he came to the very same field where his father had shot at the white deer and missed. Suddenly, from out of the undergrowth, the white deer appeared and said:

"Shoot me! If you hit me – lucky you, and if you miss – poor you!

The boy aimed and shot. He hit the deer in the heart and the deer fell down dead. The boy had no use for the carcass or for the

114

meat, but he kept the skin with the tail and legs still attached, and took it home with him, back to his mother. When he got back home, he laid the skin down and had a rest. Suddenly he sees that the deer is alive, and that his skin is covered with diamonds and pearls, which can be heard as the deer walks - like the tinkling of a glass chandelier. The son is very surprised. The mother and son decide to keep the deer in their home with them and they look after him carefully. Meanwhile, the diamonds and pearls keep dropping from the deer's skin, like leaves from a tree, and within a week the whole room is full of them. The hunter's son became very rich and he built castles as if he were a king. Eventually the son says to his mother:

"Mother why do we need all this wealth if we can't show it to people and have to keep it a secret? Let's invite the king and show him what we have."

"No, don't invite the king, because he won't bring any kindness to us."

But the son didn't listen.

"Despite what you say, I'm inviting him anyway."

"Do what you want to do then!" said the mother and she prepared a wonderful dinner for the special occasion. The son got dressed in his fancy new clothes and went to the palace to invite the king. He managed to bring the king back home with him, wined and dined him, and then showed him the deer. The king's eyes filled with envy as he watched it.

"I will take that deer with me," said the king. The boy refused to let him have it initially, but in the end had no choice. The king and his men took it by force and left.

And the hunter's son was powerless to do anything about it. Some time passed and one day the king asked for the hunter's son to be brought to him. The son goes to the king and the king says:

"These rooms are full of diamonds and pearls (four of the rooms were full and the fifth room was half full). You have to build such houses for me that nobody has ever seen the like of before."

The boy got worried when he heard this and said to the king:

"Your Excellence, I'm neither a builder nor a carpenter, and have none of the other skills required to accomplish such a feat."

"I don't care, you have to build them," said the king. "And that's that!

The boy thought for a while and then said:

"OK. Bring me two hundred cartloads of sand and two hundred cartloads of cement and I'll see what I can do."

He was given what he asked for. The boy knew a lake of alis (demons in the form of beautiful women). Whole army of alis used to drink water from that lake. The hunter's son covered the sides and the bed of the lake with the cement to make it water-tight, and then added ground cannabis resin to the water.

The alis came, drank the water, and fell into a deep trance. And the hunter's son and his men could then see all their teeth. They extracted the teeth of the alis while they lay there oblivious to everything that was going on, loaded them on to the carts, and the boy then employed a team of skilled workers to build the houses the king had requested from them. And the workers built such a house from the teeth on the cart that when the king saw it he fell unconscious. It took some time to bring him round, after which he was escorted back to his castle again.

Now among his servants there was one old man who went to the king and said:

"Your Excellency, don't waste your time. The boy seems very capable so ask him to bring you the daughter of the king of the east!"

The king ordered the hunter's son to come to him and said:

"You have to go and bring me the daughter of the king of the east!"

The hunter's son says:

"Your Excellency, if you want me to bring her to you, first you need to give me a thousand different colored pieces of silk brocade and you also need to build a ship for me."

The king gave him so many different colored pieces of silk brocade that if you looked at them your eyes would go funny. The boy loaded them on to his ship and then sets sail, just as he said he would do.

When he had been at sea for some time, he hears claps of thunder. He looks out and sees that a white hawk is after a dove and trying to catch it. The dove flies towards the ship.

"Don't let him take me," the dove pleads for help.

"Give the dove to me and I'll be very useful for you," says the white hawk to the hunter's son.

The boy gives the dove to the hawk and then continues on his way. After some time he hears a terrifying splashing sound, and sees that a white fish is swimming after a red one. The red fish jumps on board and the white fish says to the hunter's son:

Give the red fish to me and I'll be very useful for you.

The boy gives the red fish to the white fish and continues on his way once again.

He traveled a short distance or a long distance until he came to the home of the woman – the daughter of the king of the east. He took out all his colorful pieces of silk brocade at the front door of the woman. She came out and started to look at the silks. The boy told her:

"Kalbatono [Miss], these are

nothing compared to what I have on board of my ship. You can come with me and have a look if you wish." He tricked her that way. For once she had boarded the ship, he immediately set sail on the journey back.

On the way, the woman said:

"Why is that you don't have any lights on the ship? Without lights you can't see a thing in the sky."

The hunter's son strikes the top of the ship; the woman transformed herself into a dove and flew away. The boy was left empty-handed. He continued sailing, however, and very soon the white hawk brings the dove, in other words the king's daughter, back to him again. They sailed a long way and at the end the woman says:

"If you won't show me the sky, could at least you show me the waves of the sea then?"

This time the boy strikes the bottom of the ship; the woman is standing by the railings and watching the sea. This time she transforms herself into a fish and disappears from sight, plunging down to the depths of the ocean. The hunter's son is very upset but there is nothing he can do about it, so he sets sail once again. Just then he sees that the white fish that he helped earlier is bringing the fish back to him. On her return, the woman asks him:

"Who do you want me for?"

"For the king," says the boy.

"I'm not going to marry the king," says the woman. "I want you to become my husband instead and then I'll be your wife."

"How can that happen? The king will take you from me!"

"I know how to do that," replied the woman. "You only need to take him what I give you and tell him that it's a present from me, and that he and his servants need to open it together."

The hunter's son took what she gave him, went to the king, and this is what he said:

"This is a present for you from the daughter of the king of the east. You and your servants need to open it together." He said this and then quickly moved away from them. The king and his servants started to open the present when suddenly it burst open and everyone died, leaving the whole kingdom for the hunter's son, and also the woman whom he married.

I left worries there
And brought joy here,
I left the siftings there
And brought the flour here.

(Taken from Virsaladze, E. (1984) *Folktales of the World: Georgian Folktales*, Tbilisi: Nakaduli Publishing).

Contrary to what one might expect, fairy stories are not necessarily "safe" in that they frequently confront the child with the basic human predicaments we inevitably have to face in life. For example, many such tales start with the death of a parent, as this particular story does, thus creating the most agonizing problems just as it would in real life (see Bettelheim, 1991, p.8).

The story makes mention of a lake frequented by alis. An ali is an evil soul that is said to haunt travelers, pregnant women, infants, etc. Alis were both female (alkali) and male, had a wicked-looking appearance (except for the females, who were beautiful and tempting) and lived in remote woods, caves or ruins.

As for the deer, it is an animal that appears frequently in Georgian mythology. For example, the Milky Way is known as the "Leap of the Deer" and the animal even appears in the ancient Georgian hagiography, *The Life of St. Nino* (St. Nino was the first to preach Christianity to Georgians). Thus at King Mirian's orders, the crosses are made from a wondrous tree. Hunters tell the king's messengers: "If an arrow hits a deer, it hastily rushes to the foot of the hill on which this tree stands, speedily eats the fallen seed of that tree and avoids death" (Lerner, 2000, p.67). As for the antlers, they provide a means of accessing the Upper World in the same way as the Tree of Life can be used for the purpose.

It is interesting to observe that the deity described in some modern Pagan mythologies as the Celtic God of Winter, Cernunnos, also has antlers growing from his head. Cernunnos is said to have been responsible for deciding which creatures should survive the colder months and which creatures were to be culled. He was therefore also seen as the leader of the Wild Hunt and guardian of ways to the Otherworld.

It should be pointed out, however, that he is only recorded on a single inscription from Paris, where his name is uncertain and his functions unknown, and although some archaeologists have suggested the existence of a "Cernunnos type" of figure in eastern France in pagan times, this has not been confirmed and remains nothing more than speculation. The most famous representation of the God is believed to be what can be found on an artifact called the Gundestrup Cauldron. It is said to show him holding a torc (a Celtic symbol of nobility), and a ram-horned serpent, indicating mastery over animals. The figure is sitting in a cross-legged position, which is associated with both hunters and shamans. With mastery over the animals being a common attribute of shamans, there could therefore appear be a link between what has popularly become known as the Celtic God of Winter and shamanism.

Though there is no conclusive evidence to prove there is any connection between Cernunnos and the image of the stag in Georgian folktales, or even whether Cernunnos ever in fact existed, perhaps the suggestion is not as far-fetched as it might at first seem to be. Sir Fitzroy Maclean, referring to the diversity of languages and cultures that can be found within Georgia, makes the following observation: "There are even, if you know where to look for them, Celts who play the pipes and dance reels and have other Highland habits, and the tombstones in the old graveyards bear the same intricate ribbon patterns as in our own Western Isles" (Maclean, 1976, p.12). Unfortunately, however, he provides no concrete evidence to support his case.

The antlers of the stag provide the means to access the Upper World in place of the tree or the mountain that is often used for this purpose (see the story of *Davit* in Berman, 2007, for example).

They bring to mind the woodcut of the Tungus (Evenk) shaman from Nicolas Witsen's *Noord en Oost Tartaryen* (1692) that is reproduced in Alby Stone's book. The shaman in the picture is portrayed as wearing a headdress with antlers attached to it. And such headdresses have also been found at the Mesolithic site of Star Carr in Yorkshire (see Aldhouse-Green, 2005, fig.1 for an illustration).

Other examples include the depiction of the stag-man that can be found in the Camonica Valley in northern Italy, an antlered "matchstick man" incised on a panel at Pian Cogno, and a dancer from Paspardo in the same region. Similar beings also appear on a silver coin from the British Midlands, dated to about AD 10 (see Aldhouse-Green, 2005, pp.128-129, & 200). As to whether the depictions of antlered people represent ritualists wearing antler headdresses, the stages of the shaman's journey to becoming an animal during deepening trance-experience, characters in a non-shamanic mythology, or possibly just people in hunting disguises, we have no way of knowing for sure. And even the Aldhouse-Greens themselves "doubt that it is possible to argue backwards with confidence, from our understanding of the modern brain to infer the context of the earliest art and the nature of the belief systems of the earliest modern humans" (Aldhouse-Green, 2005, p.23). Nevertheless, all the evidence would seem to suggest a strong likelihood of some kind of shamanic connection cannot be ruled out.

Although using the antlers of the deer as a means of accessing the Upper World is a method of ascent that is commonly found in Georgian tales, there are of course many other ways of getting there too:

… stairs are only one of the numerous symbolic expressions for ascent [cf. the story of Jacob's Ladder from the Old Testament for an example of this]; the sky can be reached by fire or smoke, by climbing a tree or a mountain, or ascending by way of a rope, or vine, the rainbow, or even a sunbeam, for example. Finally, we must mention another group of myths and legends related to the theme of ascent – the "chain of arrows." … A volume would be required for an adequate exposition of these mythical motifs and their ritual implications (Eliade, 1964, pp.490-491).

A frequent motif in shamanic journeys is that of a tree or ladder connecting earth and heaven. Vitebsky describes how "the European story of *Jack and the Beanstalk* closely resembles a Yakut shaman's rescue of the woman abducted as a prospective bride by the raven-headed people in the sky … The main difference is that, as we now tell it, this story is not the foundation of a society and a system of morality" (Vitebsky, 2001, p.50). Instead it is told as a fairy tale to entertain children.

Eliade saw the ladder as a means of giving "plastic expression to the break through the planes necessitated by the passage from one mode of being to another, by placing us at the cosmological point where communication between Heaven, Earth and Hell becomes possible" (Eliade, 1952, p.50). He referred to "the nostalgia for Paradise", the innate desire we all have to transcend our everyday lives, and to recover the divine condition that a Christian would say existed before the Fall. The powerful motivation to pursue Paradise regained, the religious impulse, can be equated with the longing we all have to rediscover the sense of peace and union we once experienced inside our mothers' wombs (see Feinstein and Krippner, 1988, p.48).

It has been proposed that "the mystical experience, in whatever religion it may be cradled, always implies a celestial ascension" (Eliade, 1991, p.166). However, within cultures where shamanism is practiced, mystical experiences are also possible through journeys to what are known as the Lower World and the Middle World. Eliade's hypothesis, based on the Judeo-Christian concept of Heaven and Hell, would thus seem to be flawed.

A feature of initiatory patterns is when they start to lose their ritual reality they tend to became literary motifs. They then deliver their spiritual message on a different plane of human experience, by addressing themselves directly to the imagination through the medium of the story – through the journey of the hunter's son in this particular tale. For example, what can be regarded as a shamanic journey to the Upper World can be found in *Deutsche Marchen seit Grimm* (*The Princess in the Tree*), which was analyzed by Jung. The reason for this would seem to be that such initiatory scenarios answer a deep need in us. We all want to be able to experience danger, thrills and excitement, if not in reality then at least on the level of our imaginative lives (see Eliade, 2003, p.126). And this is as true now as it was in the past, as can be seen from the books that become bestsellers in our own times, and also from the films that become the biggest "Box Office Hits".

"In Jungian myths the hero, who can similarly be divine or human, is ego consciousness, which in the first half of life must defeat the unconscious out of which it has emerged and which in the second half of life must return to the unconscious and reconcile itself with it" (Segal, 1998, p.29). This is what the hunter's son can be said to achieve in this tale.

Let us now consider the use of cannabis resin. Shamans enter trancelike states that give them access to other worlds in a variety of ways. One way is by ingesting entheogens (psychoactive substances used in a religious or shamanic context), which have long been regarded as integral tools for achieving insight and epistemological understanding, and to enter modes of thought conducive to physical and psychological healing. Another common method of inducing a trance state is listening to the regular and repetitive beating of a drum – a method favored in particular by neo-shamanic practitioners. Other methods widely practiced include various forms of isolation and self-denial, such as fasting, solitary confinement, celibacy, dietary restrictions, walking pilgrimages between sacred places, rigorous regimes of immersion and bathing in ice-cold water, walking over red hot embers, and protracted prayer.

In Siberia the preferred psychoactive substance has been the mushroom known as *Amanita muscaria* or agaric. Examples of entheogens from ancient sources include: Greek: kykeon; African: iboga; Vedic: soma, amrit. Entheogens have been used in a ritualized context for thousands of years. Hemp seeds discovered by archaeologists at Pazyryk suggest early ceremonial practices by the Scythians occurred during the 5th to 2nd century BC, confirming previous historical reports by Herodotus. And the fact that the drug was known and used in the Caucasus is confirmed in this particular tale, in which it is used to induce sleep among the alis and to act as an anesthetic, enabling the king's son to extract all their teeth without them even stirring.

The formulaic opening and ending to the tale mark it out as being distinctly Georgian, as does the way in which the distance traveled is unclear, another feature that is found in many of the

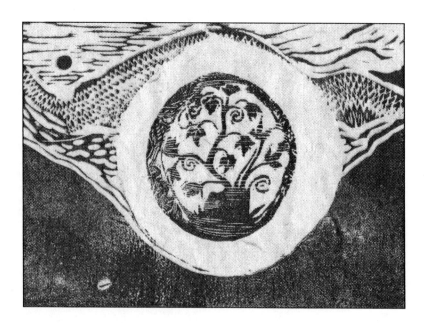

tales from the region: "He traveled a short distance or a long distance until he came to the home of the woman". And the way in which the boy understands the language of the animals and is able to communicate with them – the white deer, the white hawk, the dove, the white fish, and the blue fish – mark him out as having special abilities and being different from others, as does the ingenious way in which he is able to achieve the tasks he is set by the king. Together with the introduction of the supernatural beings (the alis), and the shape-shifting of the daughter of the king of the east, into a white dove and then into a fish, all these features suggest that once again the origin of the tale can be traced back to a time when shamanism was prevalent in the land.

Bibliography

Aldhouse-Green, M. & Aldhouse-Green, S. (2005) *The Quest for the Shaman: Shape-shifters, Sorcerers, and Spirit-Healers of Ancient Europe*, London: Thames & Hudson.

Berman, M. (2007) *Soul Loss and the Shamanic Story*, Newcastle: Cambridge Scholars Publishing.

Bettelheim, B. (1991) *The Uses of Enchantment*, London: Penguin Books.

Eliade, M.. (1989) *Shamanism: Archaic techniques of ecstasy*, London: Arkana (first published in the USA by Pantheon Books 1964).

Eliade, M. (1991) *Images and Symbols*, New Jersey: Princeton University Press (The original edition is copyright Librairie Gallimard 1952).

Eliade, M. (2003) *Rites and Symbols of Initiation*, Putnam, Connecticut: Spring Publications (originally published by Harer Bros., New York, 1958).

Feinstein, D., and Krippner, S. (1988) *Personal Mythology: The Psychology of Your Evolving Self*, Los Angeles: Jeremy P. Tarcher, Inc.

Lerner, C. (2000) *The Conversion of Kartli*, Trans. into Hebrew, comments by C.B.Lerner, Jerusalem: Magnes Press.

Maclean, Fitzroy (1976) *To Caucasus, the end of all the earth*, London: Cape.

Segal, R.A. (1998) Jung on Mythology, London: Routledge.

Stone, A. (2003) *Explore Shamanism*, Loughborough: Heart of Albion Press.

Vitebsky, P. (1993) "Shamanism as Local Knowledge in a Global Setting: from Cosmology to Psychology and Environmentalism", a paper presented at the ASA IV Decennial Conference.

The Cult of Wasterzhi & Hetag's Grove

First of all, some background information on Ossetia and the Ossetians. (The source for much of this information was North Ossetia-Alania-Wikipedia, the free encyclopedia en.wikipedia .org/wiki/North_Ossetia-Alania [accessed 22/6/08].)

North Ossetia-Alania is one of the sovereign republics of the Russian Federation and is situated on the northern slopes of the central Caucasus between two of the highest mountain peaks in Europe, Elbrous (5613m) and Kazbek (5047m). It is one of the smallest, most densely populated and multi-cultural republics, with an area of 8,000 square kilometers (3,088.8 sq ml), and a population of 710,275 in 2002, representing about 100 different nationalities.

As for the people, they are "the distant descendants and last representatives of the northern Iranians whom the ancients called Scythians and Sarmatians and who, at the dawn of the Middle Ages, under the name of the Alani and Roxolani, made Europe quake with fear" (Bonnefoy, 1993, p.262).

The ancestors of the Ossetians were the Alans, and the Daryal Gorge takes its name from them ("Dar-i-Alan", Gate of the Alans). They wandered as nomads over the steppes watered by the Terek, Kuban and Don Rivers until the Huns, under Attila, swept into Europe and split them into two parts. One group of the Alans moved into Western Europe; along with another wandering people, the Vandals, they passed through Spain into North Africa, where they disappear from history (Pearce, 1954, p.12).

The other group were forced southwards and eventually settled along the Terek, immediately north of the main Caucasus Range. There they entered into trading and cultural relations with other people of the Black Sea region, and in the tenth century were converted to Christianity. "[T]hough they did not

127

in this period attain to a written literature, the Ossetians evolved a remarkable saga, passed down orally from generation to generation-the saga of the Narts, semi-mythical heroes, something like King Arthur's Knights" (Pearce, 1954, p.12).

The vast epic cycle of the Narts is noteworthy in several respects, in particular as it is probably the last great European epic still alive and flourishing today. Not only that, but it also provides us with entire sections of a mythology that would otherwise have been lost to us.

The Narts are heroes of the past, simultaneously earthly and miraculous, who are distinguished by supernatural qualities (steel body, magic power, superhuman strength, etc.) but who lead the same daily lives as Caucasian warriors with their houses, customs, and passions. Like them, they love to talk and fight, and divide their time among feasts, raids, and war, the very image of the northern Caucasus before the Russian conquest. The Nart epic is as richly represented among the Circassians and the Abkhazians as it is among the Ossets ... But its Ossetic, even Indo-European, origin is beyond doubt (Bonnefoy, 1993, p.263).

In the last years of the Soviet Union, as nationalist movements swept throughout the Caucasus, many intellectuals in the North Ossetian ASSR called for the revival of the name of Alania, a medieval kingdom of the Alans, ancestors of the modern-day Ossetians. The term "Alania" quickly became popular in Ossetian daily life, so much so that in November 1994, "Alania" was added to the official name, which became the Republic of North Ossetia-Alania.

The population of North Ossetia today is predominantly Christian with a large Muslim minority, speaking Ossetic and Russian. According to the 2002 Census, Ossetians make up 62.7% of the republic's population. Other groups include Russians (23.2%), Ingush (3.0%), Armenians (2.4%), Kumyks (12,659, or 1.8%), Georgians (10,803, or 1.5%), Ukrainians (0.7%), and Chechens (3,383, or 0.5%). Despite the predominant religion being Russian Orthodox Christianity, followed by Islam, many of the native rituals predate both faiths.

The most popular element of the animist-pagan tradition is the cult of Wasterzhi and his sacred grove about 30 kilometers from the capital Vladikavkaz. Part protector of warriors and travelers, part phallic symbol, Wasterzhi is a mysterious character whose origins have been linked to Indo-Iranian sun worship, star worship, war gods and the ancient Nart heroes of the Caucasus. A painting often seen reproduced on posters depicts him as a medieval knight with a long beard on a white stallion with sizeable testicles.

Hoping to fully convert the Ossetians, the Russian Orthodox Church encouraged Christian saints as replacements for Wasterzhi and the rest of the extensive pagan pantheon, headed by Khusaw, the Almighty. But instead of abandoning their gods, the Ossetians fused them with the saints, creating hybrid deities subservient to Khusaw and Christianity's God. Wasterzhi's alter ego was Saint George, and Wasilla, the god of harvests and thunder, became interchangeable with Saint Illya.

"No priests are required in the popular Ossetian faith. Against a background of heavy feasting and many religious vodka toasts, Ossetian families and villages will sacrifice sheep and bulls to these lesser divinities and implore their help" (Smith, 2006, p.81). The first toast is always to the head god, who is known as "Khutsauty Khutsau ('god of gods'), or simply Khutsau, like Ancwa among the Abkhasians or Morige among the Georgians, does not intervene directly in human affairs but delegates his powers to minor deities" (Bonnefoy, 1993, p.262).

The legend behind the sacred grove outside Vladikavkaz is that a certain Hetag was fleeing his enemies in the 14th to 16th centuries when Wasterzhi called out from the mountain forest and told him to shelter there. Exhausted, Hetag collapsed on the plains, saying he could not go on, whereupon a clump of

trees (today's wood) miraculously came down and hid him. ...
Ever since, the grove has been a living cathedral for Wasterzhi,
a memorial to Hetag, and an open-air chapel for Saint George.

[T]he wood, best known as Hetag's Grove, is deeply
venerated. It is largely made up of ashes and beeches,
covering just under 13 hectares in a roughly triangular shape.
A temple with a large wooden totem pole has been built
nearby, alongside a ... banquet hall for the yearly festivals,
where each village is assigned its own tree and clearing

...Believers who pass the grove along the main road, about
a kilometre away, rise out of their seats and mumble a few
prayers to Wasterzhi, while once in the wood it is forbidden to
break off even a single branch. Holy trees are decorated with
ribbons and portraits of Saint George and the dragon. And
because of his fertility powers, women are forbidden from
saying either Hetag or the W word (Smith, pp.81-82).

When atheism was in force in Soviet times, there was a real
barrier to local traditions, but even then, the head of household
would still gather his family and pray to Wasterzhi and drink a
toast, and the tradition has both survived and flourished against
all the odds.

Despite the inevitable economic burden of a sizeable refugee
population, North Ossetia is the most well-to-do republic in the
northern Caucasus. It is the most urbanized and the most indus-
trialized, with factories producing metals (lead, zinc, tungsten,
etc.), electronics, chemicals, and processed foods. The Republic
also has abundant mineral resources and its numerous mountain
rivers serve as an important source of electric power. More than
half of the territory of the Republic is occupied by high
mountains, rich in deciduous and coniferous woods, as well as
alpine pastures.

The territory of North Ossetia has been inhabited for
thousands of years by the Vainakh tribes, being both a very fertile

agricultural region and a key trade route through the Caucasus Mountains. The ancestors of the present inhabitants were a people called the Alans, a warlike nomadic people who spoke an Iranian language. Part of the Alan people eventually settled in the Caucasus around the 7th century AD. By about the 9th century, the kingdom of Alania had arisen and had been converted to Christianity by Byzantine missionaries. Alania became a powerful state in the Caucasus, profiting greatly from the legendary Silk Road to China, which passed through its territory.

Polytheism is characteristic of the world of beliefs of nomads, and the Sarmartian Alans were no exception to this. Batraz was the Alan god of war, and there was also a mother goddess who was the equivalent of the Greek Potnia Théron. As for the cult of the Sun and the Moon, beside altars dated from the end of the 6th and the beginning of the 5th centuries BC smoking vessels have been found. It is highly likely that the people who took part in the rituals would have been overcome by the smoke produced from these vessels, and that this could have resulted in them entering altered states of consciousness, which is of course what shamans frequently did (see Vaday, 2002, pp.215-221).

The dissolution of the Soviet Union posed particular problems for the Ossetian people, who were divided between North Ossetia, which was part of the Russian SFSR, and South Ossetia, part of the Georgian SSR. In December 1990 the Supreme Soviet of Georgia abolished the autonomous Ossetian enclave amid the rising ethnic tensions in the region, and much of the population fled across the border to North Ossetia or Georgia proper. Some 70,000 South Ossetian refugees were resettled in North Ossetia, sparking clashes with the predominantly Ingush population in the Prigorodny District. That led to Ossetian-Ingush conflict.

As well as dealing with the effects of the conflict in South Ossetia, North Ossetia has also had to deal with refugees and the occasional spillover of fighting from the war in neighboring Chechnya. The bloodiest incident by far was the September 2004 Beslan hostage crisis, in which Chechen Muslim separatists of Shamil Basayev seized control of a school. In the firefight between the terrorists and Russian forces that ended the crisis, 335 civilians, the majority of them children, died.

So the Ossetes today are a divided people,

with one group (Kudakhtsy) living in South Ossetia (Georgia) and the majority living in North Ossetia (Russia). The latter are comprised of two ethnic sub-groups, Irontsy and Digortsy, each of them possessing their own dialect. North Ossetia ... was renamed 'North Ossetia-Alania' in 1994 with an aspiration to drop 'North Ossetia' at some stage, so that remaining 'Alania' would include both the South and the North (Matveena, 1999, p.89).

However, in the summer of 2008, everything changed. For on 7 August, after a series of low-level clashes in the region, Georgia tried to retake South Ossetia by force. Russia launched a counter-attack and the Georgian troops were ousted from both South Ossetia and Abkhazia. This was followed by Russia recognizing the independence of the two breakaway regions. The rest of the world, however, has not followed suit, and what the future will bring remains uncertain at this point.

Believed by scholars to descend from the ancient Scythians, the Ossetians still practise a pagan religion that has roots thousands of years old, but which has disappeared everywhere else. At the same time, Ossetians are nominally Christian. That means they stand out from the other native peoples of the multi-ethnic North Caucasus, the majority of whom are Muslim. When the Ossetians adopted Christianity, they identified Wasterzhi with the figure of St. George the Dragon-Slayer, and since the collapse of Soviet power in the Caucasus, there has been something of a revival of Wasterzhi's cult as the article that follows shows:

NORTH OSSETIA HONOURS "PAGAN" SAINT GEORGE

In their most important religious festival, North Ossetians freely mix the names of Saint George and the pagan God Uasturji - but should not drink too much vodka.

"Uastyrji, grant us your blessing," the Ossetian elder, or khistar, pronounces, whereupon everyone else seated around the festival table in the village of Khataldon last week stood up. You cannot drink to God sitting down.

"And turn off your mobile phones right now, so they do not distract us from the feast," the elder added.

The festival, known as Jiorguyba, which brings the republic of North Ossetia to a halt in the third week of November, mixes ancient and modern, pagan and Christian.

St. George is the patron saint of the festival and as in Georgia, the Ossetians mark as his feast day not the day of his death but the day he was broken on the wheel

Vasily Abayev, who compiled the etymological dictionary of the Ossetian language, finds a common root with the Ossetian form of St. George in the name of the pagan god Uastyrji.

No one hides the fact that Jiorguyba, which has been celebrated here for more than 1,000 years ever since the Alans, the ancestors of the Ossetians, converted to Christianity, has been superimposed on an even more ancient pagan rite.

In fact, St George is depicted here in Ossetia not as a 30-year-old warrior as in most of the Christian world, but as a grey-haired old man. And the information that he died a martyr for Christ, fighting a pagan king, does not bother anyone.

For centuries, the Ossetians have freely blended their pagan and Christian traditions and often it is hard to know where one tradition begins and the other ends. Uastyrji is the custodian of pagan shrines in the high valleys of the Caucasus and in the last ten years churches have been built at these sites of ancient worship.

At the turn of the last century, the German scholar of the Caucasus Gottfried Merzbacher wrote, *"In name and in their outer habits, the Ossetians are partly Muslims and mostly Christians. But in reality, both in their laws and in their religious displays ancient pagan rituals continue to predominate, which hark back to their former primitive cult."*

A hundred years on, little has changed. Modern day benefactors pray with the same zeal in both Orthodox monasteries and in the roadside shrines dedicated to pagan gods and spirits, known as zduars.

In the winter of 1992, schoolchildren in the small town of Digora reported seeing an extraordinary vision of St. George in full pagan glory, which local journalists had no qualms calling a *"milestone in the renaissance of Christianity in North Ossetia"*.

The children were playing ice hockey on a frozen river when they reported seeing a huge horseman clad in white, riding a three-legged steed, who descended from the sky onto the roof a nearby house. The apparition uttered two phrases, *"You have stopped praying to God"*, and *"Look after your young people"*.

For two weeks afterwards, the marks made by outstretched wings one and a half meters on either side, and the deep imprints of the horse's hooves, could be discerned on the roof, locals said. Snow did not fall on them and they did not melt in the sun. A church was built in Digora in honor of the vision.

Citing further proof of the single divinity of their god, mountain villagers said that both Christian and pagan shrines were spared by natural calamities this years. This summer a flood inundated all the houses in the village of Verkhny Fiagdon, but left the church of the Holy Trinity untouched. And the avalanche of ice that overwhelmed the Karmadon valley this autumn stopped just short of the shrine to Uastyrji.

"*There's no coincidence here,*" said Mikhail Gioyev, a local historian. "*Uastyrji is the favourite divinity of the Ossetians, the protector of men, travellers and warriors, but the main thing is that Uastyrji is the intermediary between God and man, people's ally, always ready to help them.*"

The beginning of the Jiorguyba festival, traditionally held on the third Sunday of November is marked by special ceremonies. In 2001, a bell-tower was dedicated in the new cathedral being built in Vladikavkaz. This year, on St. George's Day, November 24, two miracle-working icons from the town of Ivanovo were solemnly presented to the cathedral.

North Ossetia's president Alexander Dzasokhov and prime minister Mikhail Shatalov were in the congregation for the feast-day service and the priest Pavel Samoilenko read out the greetings of Patriarch Alexii II to worshippers.

"*I am really happy today,*" one of the excited worshippers, lawyer Alan Magkayev, told IWPR. "*This is a special holiday for all Ossetians. Once again we have a good reason to get drunk. If I'm serious, Uastyrji is the patron saint of men and travelers. And what is our life but a journey, which we are all traveling with faith in our hearts, sheltered by the right wing of St George?*"

It is no coincidence that the festival also falls at the end of the harvest, when the fruits have been picked and can be enjoyed. When the guests sit down at the feast, the first toast is always drunk to Khutsauty Khutsau (God of Gods) and the second is to St. George.

In every Ossetian home, three cheese pies are baked for the special day, to symbolize the union of heaven, sun and earth. In the old days, beer was specially brewed for the festival. Nowadays people get by with cans of beer and vodka is now ubiquitous - to the evident displeasure of the guardians of tradition.

"*Thoughts at the Jiorguyba feast ought to be clear and unsullied by alcohol,*" said an elder, Mairbek Gostiev. "*Otherwise a ritual full of spiritual meaning descends into general drunkenness."*

The second most important Ossetian festival is that of St. Khetaga, commemorated on the second Sunday of July, when, tradition has it, Uastyrji appeared to the Alan prince, who had converted to Christianity in the sacred grove of Khetaga.

Thousands of pilgrims flock here every year. They are strictly forbidden to talk loudly, swear or quarrel. In July 1993, a group of young men fired guns at each other in the grove. The old men could not remember a thunderstorm of the ferocity of the one that struck Vladikavkaz the next day.

"We bear collective responsibility before God for everything that happens on our earth," said archaeologist Mikhail Mamiev. *"And when someone commits a sin nearby, don't think that it doesn't concern you and don't be surprised when it affects you."*

These precepts are getting close to becoming the basis for a state religion for the North Caucasian republic. The phrase *"Uastyrji, grant us your blessing"* is now not only the beginning of a feast-day prayer but of the republican anthem of North Ossetia.

Ksenia Gokoyeva

Ksenia Gokoyeva is general director of the news organization International Information Company in Vladikavkaz.

This article was first published on 28 November 2002 (CRS No.157) by the Institute for War & Peace Reporting (IWPR), London. Articles published by the IWPR on Afghanistan, Central Asia, the Balkans, the Caucasus as well as other topics can be accessed on its website:http://www.iwpr.net

IWPR supports recovery and development in crisis zones by providing professional training, financial assistance and an international platform to independent media, human rights activists and other local democratic voices. IWPR's primary beneficiaries are local journalists who participate in its reporting, research and training programs.

Bibliography

Bonnefoy, Y. (comp.) (1993) *American, African and Old European Mythologies*, Chicago and London, The University of Chicago Press.

Matveena, A. (1999) *The North Caucasus: Russia's Fragile Borderland*, London: The Royal Institute of International Affairs.

Pearce, B. (1954) 'The Ossetians in History'. In Rothstein, A. (Ed.) (1954) *A People Reborn: The Story of North Ossetia*, London: Lawrence & Wishart. Pp.12-17.

Smith, S. (2006) *Allah's Mountains: The Battle for Chechnya*, London: Tauris Parke Paperbacks.

Vaday, A. (2002) 'The World of Beliefs of the Sarmatians'. A Nógrád Megyei Múzeumok Évkönyve XXVI.

Heart, String These Beads!

It happened and it did not happen. What can be better than God? There was a singing bird and forgiving god.

There was a king who had an only son. One day his son was playing kotchaoba (a game called "knucklebones", played with sheep's ankle-bones) with the other boys. At the same time a woman with a jug was going to fetch water from a spring. The king's son said to his friends:

"Let's bet on whether I can break that woman's jug with this stone or not."

And he threw the stone and broke her jug.

"How can I curse you? You are an only son," said the woman, "but may you fall in love with samkvertskha (three eggs) woman."

The boy went home and said to his mother:

"Mother, breast-feed me!"

"No, you're too old for that," said his mother.

But the boy kept pushing her so his mother agreed in the end, and started to breast-feed him. The boy bit the nipple he was sucking from hard with his teeth and said:

"Tell me where I can find samkvertskha woman."

His mother did not answer him so the boy bit harder. Then his mother said:

"You need to cross nine mountains, and there you will see a

138

village householder. He will give you one egg. You will leave that place and cross nine mountains again and you will see another village householder there, and you will be given the second egg. After that, when you cross nine mountains for a third time, you will be given the third egg and then you need to do as you are told."

The boy left. He walked and walked, and crossed nine mountains. At that village he was given the first egg. He crossed another nine mountains and was given another egg. He crossed nine mountains for a third time, and at the village there he was given the third egg, and was told:

"Break the other two eggs and keep this one."

The boy came to a certain spring and did as he was told. Suddenly Mzetunakhavi (a very beautiful woman) appeared in front of him. She was sitting in poplar tree, completely naked, with only a strangely beautiful looking necklace of beads round her neck.

The boy said to her:

"Stay where you are and I'll go and get you some clothes."

The boy left. At the same time an Arab woman was going to the spring. She was a clairvoyant. The Arab woman asked:

"How did you climb up into the tree? I'd like to come up too."

"I held on to the branches and climbed up that way."

"Give me your hand, and help me to climb up and join you," said the Arab woman.

Mzetunakhavi stretched out her hand to help her, but the

Arab woman threw her into the water, put her beads around her own neck, and sat on the poplar tree in her place. Mzetunakhavi was carried away by the water and drowned. Just then, the boy returned with the clothes he had gone to get. He sees, though, that the woman is dark skinned.

"What made you so dark?" he asked her.

"Waiting for you," was her reply.

"Why are your hands so dark?"

"Because I was holding my hands in front of me."

What could the boy do? He wedded her.

While all this was going on, Mzetunakhavi turned into a goldfish in the water and swam to the place where the cattle of the king's son used to drink. When the cattle went to the watering hole, the goldfish lit the water up and the cattle were so frightened that they could not drink at all. The king's son was told:

"There's something in the water that will not let your cattle drink."

So the king's son sent a fisherman to catch the fish. The fishermen caught it and put it in a golden bowl.

The Arab woman pretended to be ill. A lot of doctors were summoned but nobody could help her. Then she was asked:

"What can help you?"

"If you fry that fish and I eat it in such a way that no bone will be lost, then I will get well again, if not I'll die."

What could they do? They fried the fish, ate it, and the cooks ate it too. Then they threw the bones away. Those bones went with the rubbish and the Arab woman became well again. One of the bones ended up in front of the house of the king's son and the Arab woman, and a beautiful pear tree grew from it. The tree bore so many pears that everyone was eating them, but it just grew more and more pears. The boy said to his wife:

"Come and see what a beautiful pear tree has grown in front of our house."

Just as the Arab woman came out of her house, a big pear fell down from the tree and hit her on the head. Other pears then fell down and hit her too.

The Arab woman went back to her house and became ill again. The doctors were called but none of them could help her. Then she was asked:

"What can help you?"

"If you can cut down the pear tree in front of our house and burn it in such a way that not even one twig gets lost. Only then will I get better."

So the boy arranged for the tree to be cut down. Three twigs ended up outside the door of an old woman's house. She put two of them in the fire, but one in her cutlery drawer. When the old woman went to church to attend the services there, the twig used to turn into a woman. And, as a woman, it would sweep the floor, tidy her home, and light the fire too. The old woman was very surprised when she saw that her home was so clean and tidy, so she asked her neighbors if they knew what was going on.

"Who sweeps my floor when I go out and leave the house?"

"Why don't you hide next time and watch who does it?" they suggested.

One day the old woman got ready to go out, but instead she hid herself. The twig turned into a beautiful woman and the old woman caught her.

"Are you a Christian or a devil?" asked the old woman.

"Why should I be a devil? I'm a Christian of course."

"If so, then you can be my daughter and I'll be your mother."

"Very well. That's settled then."

And they started to live together. One day the girl said to her so-called mother:

"Can you go to the king's son for me?"

"Why not?"

Then the girl made a certain tincture, gave it to her mother, and said:

"Rub this tincture on to the backs of the king's horses."

The old woman took the tincture and did as she was asked, and the tincture the girl had made caused worms and mange to appear on the horses' backs.

The stable lads were very surprised because they did not have any clue what disease this was. They did their best to treat the horses, but none of the products they tried seemed to help.

Then the girl told the old woman:

"Go, mother, and tell the king's son that you can cure his horses. Ask him for 10 tumani and he will give you five. Take the money, and then come back here."

The old woman did as she was told. The king's son gave her 5 tumani and she brought the money home with her. The young woman then made up a different tincture, gave it to her and said:

"Now go and rub this on to the horses' backs."

The old woman did so and the horses became healthy again.

Then the necklace of the King's wife broke, the beads came off it, and nobody was able to string them back on. The young woman said to the old one:

"Go, mother, and tell the king that you can restring the beads for 20 tumani, and he will give you 10. Take the money and bring it home with you."

The old woman went to the king and said:

"I can restring your beads, but you must give me 20 tumani for it."

The old woman was given 10, she took it, and then returned home again. The king's son decided to follow her this time to see who would do the job for her as he knew she could not possibly do it herself. So he went and hid himself behind the door. The young woman realized that he was there and started to tell her life story, and this is what she said:

"I was samkvertskha woman, heart, string the beads! I was sitting in a poplar tree, heart, string the beads! I was completely, naked, heart string the beads! My husband went to bring clothes

142

for me, heart, string the beads!"

And all the time she was telling her story, the beads were restringing themselves.

"Meanwhile, while my husband was away, a woman came to me and asked me how I had managed to get into the tree. I told her with the help of the branches, heart, string the beads!"

The beads were continuing to restring themselves, and the king's son was very surprised - both by what he was hearing, and also by what was taking place before his eyes as the young woman spoke.

"Then she climbed halfway up the tree and asked me to give her my hand, heart, string the beads! She threw me into the water, heart, string the beads! The king's son came and asked her how she got so dark-skinned. She answered that waiting for him had made her turn dark, heart string the beads! He asked why her hands were dark too. She replied it was because she had kept her hands in front of her, heart, string the beads! What could the king's son do? So he wedded her, heart, string the beads! After that I turned into a goldfish and swam to where the king's son's cattle use to drink water. The cattle couldn't drink the water anymore because of me, heart, string the beads! The king's son was told that his cattle couldn't drink the water, heart, string the beads! The king's son then sent his fishermen. They caught me and put me in a golden bowl, heart strings the beads!"

Both the old woman and the king's son, not surprisingly, are finding it difficult to believe what they are hearing.

"The Arab woman got ill; a lot of doctors came but nobody was able to help her. Then she was asked what would help her but she lied, heart, string the beads! The Arab woman said that if you cook that fish and eat it in such a way that no bone gets thrown away she would live; otherwise she would die, heart string the beads! I was killed and given to the cooks. I was cooked, heart string the beads! I was eaten but one bone was thrown away with the rubbish, heart, string the beads! From this

bone such a pear tree grew that everyone was eating my fruit. And the more they ate, the more fruit the tree produced, heart, string the beads! Then the king's son called his wife to come out and have a look at the pear tree in front of their house, heart, string the beads! And when she came out I dropped pears on her head, heart, string the beads!"

The beads were continuing to restring themselves, and she took up her story once again:

"The Arab woman got ill, heart, string the beads! A lot of doctors came but once again not one of them could help her. Then she was asked what would help her. She answered that if they could cut down the pear tree so that not even one twig got thrown away she would recover; otherwise she would die. Heart, string the beads! They cut down the pear tree. Three twigs were thrown away and ended up in front of the old woman's house. The Arab woman got better, heart, string the beads. The old woman burnt two twigs and put one in her cutlery box, I turned into a woman. Heart, string the beads! Each time she went out, I was coming out of the box, cleaning, and tidying her house, heart, string the beads! And then, before she returned, I would turn back into a twig once again, heart, string the beads!"

The woman finished her story and the beads were restrung. She gave the necklace to the old woman to take home with her.

As soon as the old woman left, the king's son came out from hiding, embraced and kissed her. He married her and they celebrated by having an enormous wedding reception to which everyone was invited. As for the Arab woman, she was tied to the back of a horse and dragged through the streets that way until she was dead.

(Taken from Virsaladze, E. (1984) *Folktales of the World: Georgian Folktales*, Tbilisi: Nakaduli Publishing).

As a Christian religious symbol, a broken jug represents a loss of innocence, in particular lost virginity. And in the Old Testament Jeremiah 19 we have the Lesson of the Broken Jug. A potter's clay jug is shown to the Kings of Judah and residents of Jerusalem at the entrance to the Potsherd Gate to warn them of the disaster that will befall them, of how the Valley of Hinnom will be turned into the Valley of Slaughter, to punish them for worshipping and making sacrifices to Baal and other gods: "In this same way I'll break this people and this city, just as someone breaks a potter's vessel which he then cannot put back together again." The broken jug is thus a symbol of destruction, something that cannot be repaired. However, perhaps the most helpful insight into the significance of the broken jug is to be found in the following quote from an article by Ian Ganassi. In it he refers to an essay by Martin Heidegger entitled "The Thing" (*Das Ding*), which is collected in *Poetry, Language, Thought* (1971).

The essay uses the example of a jug, and analyzes what makes the jug a "thing" in Heidegger's special sense, rather than a mere object. ... Heidegger argues that the jug as "thing" is, in the truest sense, a "gathering": the sum total of everything associated with it—its physical composition and its human meanings and uses. Specifically, it unites ("gathers") earth (it is made of clay, and contains, and is used to pour out, water or wine, all of which are products of the earth), sky (the water or wine and the clay of the jug are products of the sun and rain), divinity (when the jug is used to pour libations to the gods), and mortals, or humans, in the combination of the previous three aspects. Heidegger argues that because our worldview has become largely a scientific one, we are deprived of the "thingness of things." It takes a special effort to get back to this true sense of "thingness" (Ganassi, I., 2006, Fragments of the Jug: Mark Strand's "The Dreadful Has Already Happened". In *Octopus Magazine*, Issue 9 http://www.octopusmagazine.com/issue09/ganassi.htm [accessed 3/1/09]).

From this it can be seen that the broken jug not only represents loss of virginity or innocence, but the way in which something can be robbed of its ethical or spiritual essence.

In *Heart, String These Beads*, by intentionally breaking the woman's jug, and by not respecting her or recognizing the importance to her of what she was trying to do, the king's only son creates disequilibrium within the community, and all the problems that follow in the tale.

A *sorcerer* can be defined as a person claiming magical powers, a practitioner of sorcery; a wizard, or a magician. The word comes from the Latin word *sortiarius*, meaning one who casts lots, or one who tells the lot of others. However, in Dan. 2:2 it is the rendering of the Hebrew *mekhashphim*, and refers to men who professed to have power with evil spirits. We also know from the Bible that the practice of sorcery resulted in severe punishment so it clearly has negative connotations. Attempts have been made to draw a distinction between someone like Carlos Castaneda, who has been labeled "a sorcerer", with its negative connotations, and shamans who do not act in such ways. It has even been suggested there is a tendency for interpreters to romantically project such features of indigenous shamanism "into otherworldly, metaphorical, meta-empirical, neutralized (or otherwise unreal) psychodrama" (Harvey, 2003, p.14). The reality is there is no such clear dividing line between the two and shamanic techniques are not always safe or necessarily conducted without malevolent designs against other persons or communities that are considered to be a threat, and in this particular tale they are conducted against the king's only son as punishment for breaking the jug.

Lewis (2003) refers to the Evenk Tungus shamans the Soviet ethnographer Anisimov observed, the way in which they would unleash their protective spirits on their enemies and how, in retaliation, their enemy would let loose a host of their own guardian spirits to do battle in the form of zoomorphic monsters – another example of the less palatable aspects of shamanism, as far as those who want their shamanism sanitized are concerned.

Let us now consider the importance of the string of beads. Ambivalence is to be found in all the magico-religious use of knots and bonds, or necklaces of beads for that matter. "The knots bring about illness, but also cure or drive it away; nets and knots can bewitch one, but also protect one against bewitchment; they can both hinder childbirth and facilitate it; they preserve the newly born, and make them ill; they bring death, and keep it at bay" (Eliade, 1991, p.112). Additionally, they also remind us of how "In the Cosmos as well as in human life, everything is connected with everything else in an invisible web; and [how] ...certain divinities are the mistresses of these "threads" which, constitute, ultimately, a vast cosmic "bondage" (Eliade, 1991, p.114). In *Heart, String These Beads*, the restoration of the equilibrium of the community only becomes possible once the broken thread of beads is restrung, and the "web" or "thread" on which every mortal life is strung is made whole again. .

As is the case in a number of stories in this collection, *Heart, String These* Beads features shape-shifting, with Mzetunakhavi turning into a goldfish and also a twig, and once again the numbers three and nine play an important part in the tale too, with there being three eggs, three twigs, and nine mountains. What we also find is that the focus is very much on the action rather than descriptions of the places or characters that appear in it, which is a characteristic of Georgian folktales too. Additionally, the fact that characters do not have names is commonplace in stories from the Caucasus, with the hero here being known as "the king's only son", and the sorcerer as "the Arab woman".

The story speaks to the unconscious of the listener, gives body to his unconscious anxieties, and relieves them, without this ever coming to conscious awareness. A shamanic journey can have a similarly therapeutic effect and both can thus be seen to have the power to heal. It is interesting to note that fairy tales were apparently used in traditional Hindu medicine to help the psychologically disoriented:

It was expected that through contemplating the story the disturbed person would be led to visualize both the nature of the impasse in living from which he suffered, and the possibility of its resolution. From what a particular tale implied about man's despair, hopes and methods of overcoming tribulations, the patient could discover not only a way out of his distress but also a way to find himself, as the hero of the story did (Bettelheim, 1991, p.25). Knowledge of the healing power of the story is nothing new and therefore its use for this purpose should come as no surprise.

When unconscious material is to some degree permitted to come to awareness and worked through in imagination, its potential for causing harm – to ourselves or others – is much reduced; some of its forces can then be made to serve positive purposes.

Bibliography

Bettelheim, B. (1991) *The Uses of Enchantment*, London: Penguin Books.

Eliade, M. (1991) *Images and Symbols*, New Jersey: Princeton University Press (The original edition is copyright Librairie Gallimard 1952).

Harvey, G. (ed.) (2003) Shamanism: A Reader, London: Routledge.

Lewis, I.M. (2003 3rd Edition) *Ecstatic Religion: a study of shamanism and spirit possession*, London: Routledge (first published 1971 by Penguin Books)

The Epilogue: Ethnic Jokes People Tell About Themselves

There are jokes some folks tell to demean other folks, such as Polish jokes told by Americans. They tell you more about the mean-spiritedness of the teller than they do about the national characteristics of the Poles.

Then there are jokes people tell on themselves, about their own kind of people. Those jokes are strangely revealing. They say something about how nations think of themselves, how they compare themselves with others, what they are proud of, and what they are willing to poke fun at.

For example, there's an old story repeated in many variations all over Europe. The last time I heard it, told by a Swiss [person], it maligned and praised five European countries simultaneously:

In Heaven the cooks are French, the lovers are Italian, the mechanics are German, the police are British, and the whole place is run by the Swiss. In Hell the cooks are British, the lovers are Swiss, the mechanics are French, the police are German, and the whole place is run by the Italians.

An Asian version of this joke was told to me by a Chinese woman. Apologies in advance to American feminists, but this is how the Chinese tell it:

In Heaven the food is Chinese, the women are Japanese, and the houses are American. In Hell the houses are Chinese, the food is Japanese, and the women are American.

Cardinal Paulo Evaristo Arns of Sao Paulo tells this one: We have an old political joke in Brazil. We were at the brink of an abyss and now we have taken a great step forward.

The Austrians have lots of jokes that emphasize how disorderly and happy-go-lucky they are compared to their Teutonic neighbors. For instance: The Prime Ministers of Germany and Austria met to exchange notes. "How are things in Germany?"

asked the Prime Minister of Austria. The German sighed, "Well, in Germany the situation is serious," he said, "but not hopeless." "In Austria the situation is hopeless," the Austrian Prime Minister replied, "but not serious."

Some nations have jokes about their own internal divisiveness, such as this one from India: "One Indian is worth two Chinese. Two Indians are worth one Chinese. Three Indians are worth nothing."

Another one comes in many versions, but I first heard it from a Dutchman. Holland has more than twenty feisty political parties, and my own experience of the Dutch is that they would rather cooperate with anyone else rather than another Dutchman. So I like this joke best the way they tell it in Holland:

Satan was conducting a guided tour of hell. The tour group entered a chamber with three pots of boiling oil, all full of howling people. Around one pot was a ring of devils with pitchforks, catching people who escaped from the pot and pitching them back in. Around another pot were just a few devils, haphazardly watching for escapees. Around the third pot were no devils.

"Why are there so many devils around that pot and none around this one?" asked the tourists.

"Well, there where all the devils are is the pot for the Jews," said Satan. "They keep helping each other climb out of the pot. So we need a big guard to keep throwing them back in. In the second pot are the Germans. They never help each other, but occasionally a clever one manages to pull himself out. So we have to keep a few guards there. In the third pot are the Dutch. We don't need to watch that pot. Whenever one of those fellows crawls out, the others pull him back in."

The most bitter joke about a region's inability to get along with itself comes, appropriately, from Israel.

A frog and a scorpion were sitting on the bank of the River Jordan. "Hey, frog," said the scorpion. "I need to go to the other side of the river. Would you carry me across on your back?"

"No way," said the frog. "If I let you come close to me, you'd sting me and kill me."

The scorpion said, "That would be stupid. If I stung you while we were in the river, we'd both drown."

"Hmmm, that's true," said the frog. "OK, hop on."

So the scorpion climbed on the frog's back and they headed out into the River Jordan. Halfway across the river the scorpion stung the frog.

"What did you do that for?" cried the frog, as they were both going down for the third time.

"I couldn't help it," said the scorpion. "This is the Middle East."

I suppose every nation has jokes praising itself. My favorite comes from the Soviet Republic of Georgia, on the south slopes of the Caucasus Mountains. I heard it at the most typically Georgian of occasions, a banquet at which people were drinking wine, making toasts, and singing songs about Georgia.

Just after God created the earth, he called all the peoples and nations to assemble on a certain day, so each could be presented with a homeland. All the nations dutifully showed up, except the Georgians. God parceled out a piece of the earth to each nation, and then, weary from the task, he started home. On the way he came across the Georgians, sitting on the grass under a tree, drinking wine and singing.

"Why didn't you come to the Giving of the Homelands?" God asked. "Now you have none for yourselves."

The Georgians were crestfallen. "We're sorry, God," they said. "We were on our way, but we were so impressed by the beauty of this world that we stopped to drink a toast to the grass and the trees. Then we drank toasts to the sun and to the blue waters and to the high mountains. In fact we spent the whole day here, singing and drinking to the loveliness of your creation."

God was touched. "Well," he said, "there is still one little piece of earth left, the most beautiful of all. I was saving it for myself. But since you know so well how to appreciate it, you shall have it, and it shall be called Georgia..."

BOOKS

O is a symbol of the world, of oneness and unity. In different cultures it also means the "eye," symbolizing knowledge and insight. We aim to publish books that are accessible, constructive and that challenge accepted opinion, both that of academia and the "moral majority."

Our books are available in all good English language bookstores worldwide. If you don't see the book on the shelves ask the bookstore to order it for you, quoting the ISBN number and title. Alternatively you can order online (all major online retail sites carry our titles) or contact the distributor in the relevant country, listed on the copyright page.

See our website **www.o-books.net** for a full list of over 500 titles, growing by 100 a year.

And tune in to myspiritradio.com for our book review radio show, hosted by June-Elleni Laine, where you can listen to the authors discussing their books.

MySpiritRadio